Bathing Beauties

Adam Colyer

I hope that you enjoy the book

Adam

Published by

MELROSE
BOOKS

An Imprint of Melrose Press Limited
St Thomas Place, Ely
Cambridgeshire
CB7 4GG, UK
www.melrosebooks.co.uk

FIRST EDITION

Cover by Melrose Books

ISBN 978-1-910792-11-7

Printed and bound in Great Britain by:
4edge Limited
7a Eldon Way, Eldon Way Industrial Estate
Hockley, Essex
SS5 4AD

Contents

Acknowledgements

I would like to thank Lucy Seddon for taking this all the way to Vietnam to provide a very useful proof read, Chrissie Snelling who provided the brilliant artwork for the cover and my wife, Sarah, for her support and encouragement to transfer the story idea I have to print so it can be shared and hopefully enjoyed by a wider audience. I hope you enjoy the book.

Introduction

This book is a work of fiction and the characters are not based upon anyone in particular. I am however sure that people like this exist and the good should make their stand against those who abuse power in the most absurd ways. Sometimes the best way to beat this is to find a more absurd battle plan!

I have not invented the place they call Penge, yes it really exists. Penge is in South East London and has always seemed a grim place. I used to live in Beckenham, which was nice, holding many happy memories, however next to Beckenham is Penge, where the sun forgot to shine.

If you should drive down Penge high street (do not walk if it is your first time) it will not inspire you to stop to enjoy the area further. You will be tempted to drive faster so you can leave should the constant traffic chaos allow. When you look at their faces, the residents all seem to have been given some bad news at the same time: perhaps they were reminded they still live in Penge! All the more reason why the few pleasures those in Penge may enjoy should be protected; there is also the burden of Crystal Palace being the local football club, which can be a rollercoaster of emotion for those who support it.

Part of the reason why Penge has made a mark on my life is that I used to work behind the bar at the Penge Social

Club. I enjoyed the company of the locals as they drank ever-increasing quantities of 'snakebite' (lager and cider mixed, on occasion, with blackcurrant). This was not pleasant going down and much less pleasant when it came back up. To add to the fun I worked on the nights when the club singer was on. You dream of evenings of good music and sparkling company. Oh well, the things you do for money.

Let me introduce synchronised swimming to this tale. Some may think that this must be fiction yet it actually happens. It is harmless yet seems rather pointless. Is it rational to wear make-up and sequins just to jump into a swimming pool? I am sure there are other activities, which are equally bonkers, but what makes our country great is that we are allowed to do them. It is, however, an example of an absurd misuse of power when synchronised swimming is used in a community battle between good honest people and the local council's misuse of power. Who would you like to win?

Strange as this might seem, this is the story; let the battle of the sequins commence.

1

An ordinary day

There was nothing out of the ordinary about Jim, just a regular sort of bloke getting by the best he can. Routine was the key. Jim had lost his wife two years ago and his business a year after that and he found that having a routine helped him keep going. He did not want to end up confined to his own two-bedroom flat with nothing but daytime TV for company.

Jim was well known in Penge, which was partly due to the business he ran. Jim was an ironmonger and had his own independent shop on the high street. It was the sort of shop where you would find all sorts of useful things and there was also the personal service which you just do not seem to get in the big DIY chains. It was the rise of such stores that caused shops like Jim's to call it a day, there was no way they could compete. But many of the locals, however, still remember and respected Jim. Some would say how much they missed his shop while carrying their B&Q bag.

Every morning the alarm clock would still ring at 7am and after the morning cup of tea Jim would be out of his flat and walking down Maple Road at 8.30am. This was a habit, which was hard to break, from when he used to open his shop at 9am sharp every morning – except Sundays when he went for a walk in Crystal Palace Park, early, before it got too crowded.

Thursday was market day; this was Jim's favourite day. There was always lots of activity and colour, which brought the whole area to life. There was a sense of community and Jim's spirits were uplifted as he felt he belonged. All the market traders knew Jim and they all knew his routine, they could almost set their watches by him. This did, however, mean that they were ready for him with a bit of friendly banter as he walked past.

"Here he is, Jim the Nail," a reference to his old shop and the actor (Jimmy Nail). This nickname had sort of stuck and it was guaranteed that someone would shout this out as if it were the first time and highly original. Jim was used to it and did not mind, it felt like he was part of the community, he felt accepted. On occasion someone would have thought of something new to say. This was usually greeted with an approving titter from the other market traders, "There is life here, but not as we know it, Jim." A *Star Trek* reference and quite appropriate for Penge. There was no shortage of people wanting to be jokers.

The market traders all meant well and deep down they liked Jim, he was part of the local scenery and they would miss him if he wasn't there. Well, all apart from one called William who ran a sweet stall. William was a rather reluctant stallholder, his dream was to be a children's entertainer, but this was shattered when he made national TV stardom for being the worst magic act ever at the audition stage. He was laughed off the stage and the footage has been repeated numerous times for the sheer entertainment factor. He did not appreciate the banter (which there was plenty of) and ended up not liking anybody, especially children, as he saw them as the reason for his downfall.

The locals all referred to William as 'Willy Plonker' and

would ask where his golden tickets were hidden – well, he was in the confectionary industry in his own small way. The local kids just called him ‘Plonker’. When Jim passed William’s stall the comments would be more like: “If you are looking for your shop it ain’t there no more.” This did not worry Jim.

The normal route (once past the market) would take Jim past his old shop, which is now a kebab restaurant of dubious quality. There was a strange and disturbing aroma which became stronger the nearer you got to it. This did, however, have the benefit of helping the partially sighted know where they were. The owners of this outlet had grand ideas and named the ‘restaurant’ the South London Kebab Centre. It was fortunate that the old business premises were sold at the top of the market, giving Jim something to show for his past efforts, otherwise it would be difficult to walk past. Even so nothing would tempt him in, and that was not just because of the food (although that was reason enough).

Once past the high street Jim would normally head for the house where his mother, sister and teenage nephew lived. He would like to pop in to make sure they were all OK and just generally spend time with his family, more important to him now since the loss of his wife.

This house is where Jim was brought up and he was now the only adult male influence; his father had died years ago and his sister’s ex-boyfriend now lived in Manchester with a female wrestler. The DIY skills Jim had picked up from running his business were usually called upon for various jobs around the house and his nephew looked upon him almost as a father figure.

Jim’s sister, Sharon, was happy being a single mother, the experience of being left for Busty Bianca of the Northern

Slam Fest had not left her ready for another relationship just now. Sharon turned her matchmaking skills to Jim, whether he liked it or not. Each time Jim called round it would seem that Sharon would have details of another potential match. Sometimes the date had already been arranged.

These dates hardly ever went well as Sharon was more concerned with quantity over quality and in a place like Penge this was always going to be a dangerous approach. Jim had previously met most of the 'availables' from the local Mecca bingo club but nothing had really clicked (or even 'clickety clicked').

There was once hope, however, for a lady who lived in nearby Sydenham who was lovely. She had the looks, the personality and even appeared to have some money. The problem was that she also had something else which explained why she was known locally as George. George told Jim that she was booked in for the operation and they should give it a go, but this was not going to happen.

This morning, after Jim had been given his list of jobs around the house, Sharon sat him down with another cup of tea. Jim knew what was coming and made sure he got his word in first. "Have you made sure that this one isn't a man?" Sharon assured Jim that she had been more careful this time including establishing the correct gender. "Will I know her from *The Jeremy Kyle Show* or do I find out all her problems afterwards?" Sharon admitted that some of the previous dates had not gone too well and yes, *The Jeremy Kyle Show* had previously been on the phone wanting Jim to appear to sort out a love triangle or two. "I know you mean the best for me, but why can't you leave me alone?"

Sharon was insistent, "Jim, this time I've found you a gem." Jim had heard this before and was not convinced.

Sharon continued: "She is ideal for you and my friends tell me there will be no nasty surprises this time, and you are meeting her at 7.30pm tonight!"

Jim knew he should say no, deep down he wanted to say no, but Sharon was not taking no for an answer. "Okay Sharon, I'll go, but this will be the last time if she is a man or if there are any other problems that I don't need."

"Trust me," said Sharon. "I 'ave a good feeling about this time."

"You are meeting outside The Swan; drop in here first at 6pm for something to eat."

Jim knew that the real purpose of this was to be briefed on what information she had on the 'date', which was not always very accurate from previous experience, and so that Sharon could plan his evening. Again Jim did not like this, but was powerless to say no. "She will be wearing a pink coat and her name is Tilly."

So the deal was done, he was to meet another total stranger, on the street, who appeared to dress like a prostitute, be told how to play the evening and all in a pub where a fair number of people knew him (and would delight at the entertainment of things going pear-shaped).

What could possibly go right?

2

Here we go again!

Jim had quite a lot of time to think over his ‘date’ with Tilly as he tackled the list of DIY jobs he had been given this time. Today he had been asked to investigate the central heating. Sharon issued the first task. “Some of the radiators are only hot halfway up Jim, I don’t understand it, can you ’ave a look?”

Jim kept a toolkit here, which always came in handy, and knew instantly what to do.

Within half an hour he had bled the radiators and fixed the problem. Jim was relieved at the easy fix and perhaps his ‘list’ would not be too bad today.

“Jim you are a bloomin’ star; what will we do without you when Tilly takes you off?” said Sharon. Jim replied, “I am not sure I even want to go and you have me married to the woman, if you are sure she is a woman this time.” Sharon was not going to let Jim back out.

“You are going because I won’t let you back out, you can’t let her down.”

“But you bloody arranged it,” protested Jim.

“I know I arranged it and you will NOT let her down, Jim!”

There was no point in arguing, he wasn’t going to win. Jim prepared to leave the house having to accept his life being arranged for him – ‘For his own good’.

Jim was at the point of opening the front door when Sharon called, "Jim, there is just one more thing. I've had my Barry Manilow poster framed and it needs puttin' up." Jim's heart fell, for one he had hated Barry Manilow ever since Sharon used to play his records constantly at a loud volume all the time, and secondly putting up pictures was always not as easy as it should be. Jim, however, knew he could not say no.

"So where is old big nose going then?"

"Don't call him that, he is lovely, he is a musical god. One day I'll meet him and then I will tell him about your rude comments." Sharon was very protective about 'her Barry' and had a dream he would come to Penge to whisk her away. This did not seem very likely.

So the painful picture-hanging process started.

"Right a bit, left a bit, no too much; back a bit and higher. No, not that high!"

Finally, Sharon was happy with where Barry should be mounted – in relation to the picture although she had often thought about mounting 'her Barry'.

"Yes, yes, that's where I want Barry, hold it there, Jim."

Just at that point the phone rang and Jim was left holding this damn picture until Sharon had stopped chatting to one of her bingo pals; he dare not move it now the desired place had been found. This went on and on with what Jim considered mindless chit-chat, however to Sharon these calls were important, important enough to suspend the hanging of Barry. Jim had thoughts on hanging Barry during this delay, but this was not in the same way.

Eventually the phone call ended and the picture was finished, it had pride of place in the lounge above the sofa. "Thank God it's not in 3D, I don't fancy looking up his nostrils."

"Don't be rude, Jim. I bet Tilly likes Barry Manilow," said Sharon. At that point Jim had to leave and with one further worry about how his evening would unfold.

Later that day Jim had returned home to go through the familiar process of having a bath, picking out some smart clothes and preparing for the evening ahead. He would make the effort more out of self-respect rather than any expectation that the evening would go well. There was, however, always the outside chance that something may come of it. Jim quietly held onto that hope.

Having got ready, Jim left his flat and started the familiar walk down Maple Road. By this time the market had long since packed up, there were just the tell-tale signs of the odd bits of litter and cabbage leaf which had escaped the attentions of the general clean-up. There were still a few people about and Jim stood out with his appearance and the aroma of Oasis Spice, which alerted those milling about that Jim was near even before they saw him. Oasis Spice was the aftershave Sharon had bought for him last Christmas. Jim kept using it hoping that it would run out one day and he would be rid of it, the bottle, however, seemed to be lasting forever.

The advance warning aroma had given the chance for those about to think up some comments: they had a good idea that Jim was going on another date arranged by his sister.

"I've 'erd that this one has got five kids all under the age of ten, all by different fathers, you will be knee high in puke and nappies this time."

Another commented, "Watch out, her boyfriend is in the army and will rip your balls off!"

These comments were quite close to Jim's previous experiences of Sharon's 'perfect match', however, Jim just smiled, gave a wave and carried on. He knew that he was nearly at the end of Maple Road as the smell from the South London Kebab Centre was getting stronger.

The kebab shop was not busy at this time in the evening but the spit was turning with the usual flood of grease dripping from it. "Good luck Jim, fancy a kebab?" How they could pick up the aftershave over the smells in their shop was beyond belief. Jim refused the offer of the kebab and made his way to Sharon's house.

As soon as he was in the door Sharon started to glow. "Look at you, you are gorgeous, dressed up and somewhere to go, eh! Tilly is a lucky girl, how can she resist, you are even wearing that lovely aftershave I bought you. Go on, give us a kiss you charmer you, let me just straighten your shirt, you are all wonky!"

"Oh for heaven's sake, sis, leave me alone, stop fussing. I learnt not to expect too much from these 'dates', I am not normally disappointed that way."

"This time could be different," Sharon had belief. "This could be the one and I want you to be your best."

Alerted by the noise in the hall and the aroma of the Oasis Spice, Mum knew Jim had arrived. "Jim, into the kitchen with you, let me 'ave a look at my beautiful boy." Jim's mum was called Dorothy, but was known locally as Dot and was always proud of her son. "Sharon has told me all about Tilly and she sounds just right for my Jim." This was great, his mum and sister seemed to know all about 'his intended' but Jim still did not have a clue. He was called to the table before having a chance to ask any questions, "Sit down, supper's ready, let me just call John," Sharon ordered.

"John… John… JOHN! Down 'ere now, supper's on the table, you can't keep your Uncle Jim waiting, he's on his hot date tonight," Sharon barked. Dot turned to Jim, "He's up in his room too much, doing God knows what, he also needs a nice girlfriend."

"Leave him alone, he will be alright if you just leave him alone." Jim felt quite protective of his nephew and knew how controlling his mum (and indeed sister) could be. Dot replied, "The trouble is without a nice girlfriend he is not leaving himself alone, if you know what I mean." At that point Sharon came back into the room, closely followed by John, they did not appear to have heard what Dot had just said.

"Hello Jim, ready for your night out? I've heard she's a bit raunchy, if you can't be good be careful…"

"Shut up, John, don't wind your Uncle Jim up," interrupted Sharon.

Dot looked John in the eye, "You need to sort out your own love life before you go blind!" At this point Jim had to stop them, "Look, you all seem to know about Tilly, would it be too much to ask if you told me?" This seemed to be appropriate so Sharon served up the home-made cottage pie and over supper the briefing started.

Sharon was eager to start, "She's lovely, honest, recently divorced with a grown-up kid, there are no nasty surprises, I've checked this out with the bingo girls." The bingo girls were considered to be a good source of gossip and would know if there was anything she should let Jim know about, so Sharon thought. "She wants to meet someone who is good with his hands round the house," added Dot. John sniggered. "She didn't mean like that," protested Jim, thinking that John had picked up some sort of saucy double meaning. Dot kept very quiet, leaving Jim with just an element of doubt about what she did mean.

Sharon told Jim all she knew over supper, which was not really that much once you got past the gossip, so he still did not know quite what to expect. One thing he knew for sure was that she would shortly be outside The Swan wearing a pink coat, expecting to meet him.

It was time to leave the house; the pub was not far away, just round the corner. Jim left with his family giving him a push in the right direction with the best possible intentions. He was full of apprehension, what will happen this time?

3

Meeting Tilly

Jim arrived outside The Swan in good time looking out for the promised vision in pink, feeling a little awkward and hoping that not too many people notice that he was waiting for another date. Not much chance of that and the aftershave was also a giveaway. Those who passed by noticed Jim and had a fair idea of why he was there. It was good for the pub's business as soon it was quite full of locals eagerly awaiting the arrival of Jim and his latest. This had been excellent entertainment in the past.

Ten long minutes had passed by before eventually Jim saw the bright glow of baby pink walk towards him. This was it, it must be Tilly. He thought it would be pink, but this was something else. This was certainly going to attract some attention, not much chance of hiding the whole event in a quiet corner unnoticed.

"Are you Jim?" said the pink glow.

"Yes, I'm Jim, pleased to meet you, you are looking very…" Jim knew he had to stop himself saying 'pink'. "Nice."

"I'm so glad it's you, there are a lot of strange people about tonight, but you look quite normal," Tilly replied. She had noticed Jim's scent but was too polite to say what she was thinking. "I'm a lucky girl spending the evening with you."

Jim was quite taken back by the first impressions, but managed to utter, "I thought we could have a drink in here, how does that sound?"

"That sounds lovely, Jim, let's go and have a drink."

As soon as they entered the pub the whole pub went quiet; it was difficult to miss the main event of the evening when one had the strong smell of cheap aftershave and the other was a pink glow. The silence was broken by the sound of a single dart missing the board and hitting the wood surround. "You made me miss my shot, I have never missed that board before," could be heard from the corner. This was quickly shouted down: "Leave it out, you always miss that bloody board," came another voice, which raised a laugh and broke the focus on Jim and Tilly. The general noise of the pub returned.

They moved to a spare table and must have been aware of being watched out of the corner of people's eyes as they tried to look like they were minding their own business. There was the odd comment here and there which they either did not hear or just did a good job of blocking out. "At least this one is a woman," or "I think this time he's paid for a hooker!" were examples of the locals' first impressions.

Once at the table Jim could not help notice the very blonde hair. He asked Tilly what she wanted to drink. "I'll have a dry white wine please, Jim." This was going quite well. Tilly appeared to be friendly and also rather attractive, she just needed to take off that coat as it was still drawing attention. Tilly took off her coat and sat down as Jim went to the bar to get the drinks.

As Jim approached the bar the barmaid was waiting for him open-mouthed. Before he had a chance to order the drinks the barmaid said, "Now Jim, isn't that a sight!" Jim thought she couldn't possibly mean the coat as Tilly had taken it off. "She likes her colours, doesn't she?" Jim turned round to see that Tilly was wearing a yellow top, which was every bit as bright as her coat. You could just hear a disorganised rendition of 'The sun will come out tomorrow, bet your bottom dollar…' through the general noise.

Jim returned to the table with the glass of wine and his pint of beer and was welcomed by a smile, which was brighter than the clothes she was wearing. "Thanks, Jim… as you can see I like my colours, I hope you don't mind." How could Jim answer that, but the truth was all Jim could see was that smile, he had not felt this way for a long time. Jim managed to reply, "Like I said, Tilly, you look very nice."

Before Jim had a chance to ask Tilly anything she broke the ice by saying that Sharon had told her all about him. Now this could be good or it could be bad, but Jim hoped that his sister hadn't revealed anything too embarrassing. "Don't worry, Jim, nothing too bad otherwise I wouldn't have turned up," Tilly joked. Jim was starting to feel at ease; he did not have that feeling that it was all going to go horribly wrong as he had on previous dates Sharon had arranged for him. On previous occasions Jim's date had started cat fights, danced on the table singing out of tune to 'Dancing Queen' or the emergency services had to be called out after 'the date' had got stuck trying to climb through some decorative ironwork over the bar. This time it seemed different. Jim asked Tilly, "Sharon hasn't told me much about you, all I know is that she knows you from going to bingo."

Jim was unsure where to start, should he go for the full life history? No, keep it a bit lighter, ask her how she spends her time. "Do you enjoy bingo then? I can't say I've been, what is all the fuss about those little balls then?"

"There's good prize money to be had, and it gets me out of the house. Mind you I don't go too often unlike some of them, they seem addicted to it."

"That sounds like my sister, she has her own personalised bingo marker set and swears that she will win the jackpot every time she goes."

"She's not the only one. I don't take it as seriously as that, it's a reason to go and do something and meet up with a few friends, like your sister, don't worry."

By this time the locals were beginning to lose interest in Jim and Tilly, things appeared to be going too well, where's the entertainment in that? Some were starting to leave in the hope of catching the end of *Eastenders* or something else which would provide a bit of a laugh. Others stayed on, but by now they took far more interest in their beer or gin.

"I enjoy my swimming," continued Tilly. Jim was curious.

"Swimming, where do you do that?"

"At the local baths on the road to Sydenham."

Jim was surprised: this pool was very old, he had swum there as a kid. Jim thought that it had closed down years ago. "Is that still going? I haven't been in that pool for years."

"I go every Tuesday and Friday evenings, sometimes at the weekend as well, it's a sort of club we have, I wouldn't want to miss it."

Jim was still surprised by this. "I had no idea about a swimming club in the area, do you go in for races – what happens at this club then?"

"No, no, it's not the Olympics, we just like to meet to have a bit of a swim and a bit of a chat." Before Jim had a chance to ask more Tilly continued, "It's a bit like a social club you can float about in really, the people at the pool are pleased to see us, most people now want to go to that posh pool in Beckenham with those flumes and everything. "We don't care for that, we like our little pool, it's got character."

"I remember the pool from when I was a kid," replied Jim. "'Does it still have the broken tiles and the dodgy showers?"

"Like I said, Jim: it's got character, anyway it means a lot to us to meet up, if it wasn't for the pool some of us wouldn't get out at all, we are a nice bunch if I don't say so myself."

This was a turn up for the books; the evening was going very well, no embarrassing moments or nasty surprises, just a lovely evening with Tilly, it didn't matter at all about the bright pink coat. After another couple of drinks it was a surprise how time had passed. After the barmaid called last orders, Tilly said, "Jim, is that the time? Oh my good God, I have had a really nice time tonight but I have to go, I didn't think it was that late."

As Jim helped Tilly put her pink coat on he felt he must act, he would like to see Tilly again. Jim took a breath for courage and said: "Tilly, I have really enjoyed meeting you. Is there a chance we could meet up again?"

Tilly looked Jim in the eyes, made that wonderful smile that first greeted him and said, "Why don't you come to swimming tomorrow night, we meet in the pool at half past seven."

"How will I find you, Tilly?"

"Jim, I like bright colours: you will see me, just make sure you don't wear your old Speedos, the club won't be ready for that."

That was it, it was a second date and for once Jim felt very comfortable about the prospect, he was looking forward to it. They left the pub and Jim offered to walk Tilly home. Jim hardly had enough time to say how he had enjoyed the evening before they were at Tilly's house. "Here we are then Jim, thank you for a super night, I look forward to seeing you tomorrow."

"Oh, ok then, that's great, I will have to search out my armbands, it's been quite a while." Tilly chose to overlook that rather poor attempt at humour, gave Jim a hug and simply said, "See you tomorrow," before walking up her front path.

Jim walked home as if he was on air, had Sharon finally found that someone special? It somehow felt right this time. Time would tell, but he was looking forward to revisiting that old pool after all this time.

4

The water's lovely, come on in

On Friday morning Jim had a warm feeling inside as he walked down Maple Road. It was not market day so it was much quieter, however there were still a few people about. They were waiting for Jim as word had got around about his date with Tilly.

"Here he comes, Jim the Nail, a proper little charmer, eh!" The smile on Jim's face was a giveaway that he was still pleased with how the evening went. "Look at him – he must have nailed her, the dirty rascal." Jim didn't rise to these comments, just smiled and continued walking.

Further down the road Willy Plonker was trying to wipe off the latest bit of graffiti from his stall, which had been left overnight. This time it was a reference to Stacey and what she had done on his stall with a boy from Anerley the night before. "Bloody kids, no bloody respect. I am going to sell them laxative chocolate, that will teach them." He briefly looked up to see a smiling Jim walk past. "Why are you so happy? Oh yes, I've heard about your date last night, the word is that it went far too well, spoilt everyone's evening by all accounts. I'll be wiping graffiti off my stall about you next, makes me sick. I've got to serve sherbet lemons off this!" Jim just smiled a little bit more and walked past.

As usual Jim was on his way to the house, where he knew that Sharon would be waiting, wanting to know every detail about the previous evening with Tilly. The door of the house opened before he had a chance to put his finger on the bell. "Jim, in you come, I want to hear all about it, come and sit in 'ere under my Barry." Oh yes, that bloody picture he put up, he was going to be interrogated under a giant pair of nostrils.

"I've heard that you took her home you naughty boy, I hope you behaved yourself, my friends tell me that you were getting on VERY well. You naughty boy, shouldn't you take it easy rather than like a rat up a drain pipe…"

"Sharon, I just walked her home, nothing more than that," Jim had to interrupt as Sharon was starting to get the wrong idea completely.

"I was told that you were getting on like a proper loved-up couple, is it true that her coat was that bright? I knew that I should have hidden in a corner to check up on you."

"Sharon, remember the last time when you hid behind a copy of *Hello* magazine? That wasn't very subtle."

"I would have been okay, but Tina from the bookies spotted me…"

"I knew it was you as soon as I walked in and it was embarrassing when you started that fight at the end."

"She deserved it, no one dares to cheat at my bingo club and when I saw her I lost it, anyway, it seems you liked Tilly a lot, when are you seeing her again then?"

"Tonight," replied Jim.

"TONIGHT! You are keen aren't you, where are you taking her?"

"Well, she asked me to join her at some sort of swimming club."

"Swimming club, bloody hell Jim, when did you last go swimming, be careful you don't sink, oh my God."

Dot had heard this conversation from the kitchen and

had time to go upstairs to find something. She went into the lounge with something that she thought Jim might find useful. “Jim, I’ve found your old trunks, they may be a bit small now, but you’re not shy are you?”

“Mum, I am not wearing those, they are too small and full of holes, throw them away. I’ve got some I can wear which will at least cover me up!”

“She might like to see what a big boy my Jim is.” John appeared at this point, his school was closed today due to electrical faults, the rumour being that the older pupils had vandalised the vital services again. Some thought it was the teachers so they could get a long weekend. John took one look at the trunks Dot was holding and burst out laughing. Sharon turned to John, “What are you laughing about, make yourself useful if you are home today.”

“You could find yourself a nice girlfriend, perhaps you should be wearing these!” interrupted Dot.

“Your Uncle Jim has got another hot date tonight,” added Sharon.

Dot added “He is going to dive onto Tilly at the local pool!”

“Gran, you’re wicked,” chuckled John.

“She did not mean that,” Jim protested, “Anyway, I must go now, any jobs will have to wait till next time.”

Jim did have to go; he worked as a handyman to earn enough to make ends meet, his knowledge from running his old shop being put to good use. He had a few local calls to make so made his excuses and left the house. Jim left Sharon and John arguing about how John should spend his day off school, not, as Dot added, “Up in his room wearing himself out!” adding that Sharon should turn her ‘Cilla’ matchmaking skills to him next.

Later that day Jim had finished the calls he had arranged and was back at his flat getting ready for meeting Tilly again. What should he wear? It did not really matter, he was going swimming after all, he certainly should not wear his aftershave as that might contaminate the pool! Jim did need to find his trunks though. He last bought a pair for a holiday in Spain many years ago. The good news was that he had found them and they would fit, but they were bought when he was a big fan of the group Wham, something he always thought he may regret some day, today was that day.

As Jim walked into the old pool building many childhood memories came back to him, it seemed just the same as it was years ago. The ticket office was just the same, he had to stop himself asking for a child's entry. "One adult please. Bloody hell this place hasn't changed much, it's been years since I was last here."

The attendant did not take much interest and just replied, "That's three pounds."

"Well the bloody price has certainly changed," chuckled Jim. The attendant showed even less interest, passed Jim his ticket, pointed towards the changing room and returned to her magazine, a smooth practised movement all within two chews of her gum.

The changing rooms seemed very familiar, if not a bit more run down but just being there brought more memories. Jim got changed, found a rare locker that seemed to lock properly and took the familiar route to the poolside.

The pool itself seemed just the same except it seemed virtually empty, not the noisy, busy place he remembered. It was not difficult to spot Tilly, again her smile shone through. Tilly soon spotted Jim. "Jim, nice to see you. What's that, 'Wham Bam I am a Man'. Well that's good to know, come on in and meet the gang." Jim had forgotten about his trunks and felt very embarrassed, the sooner he was in the water the better.

Tilly was in a group of six swimmers; they were just at the side of the pool discussing whatever the hot topics of the day were, occasionally breaking off to swim a length or two. As Jim approached the group Tilly welcomed him in. "Like the trunks, Jim, did you buy them for me?"

"No … I mean … I already had these … they seemed like a good idea at the time, I'm not so sure now."

"Never mind, Jim, welcome to our little club."

With Tilly were Steve, Andrew, Cath, Derek and Doris. They were all now single apart from Derek and Doris who were married and did everything together – they were known fondly as the 'double Ds'. They were quite a mixed bunch but shared the enjoyment of having a good reason to get out of the house and spend some time with friends, the pool provided the ideal venue.

There was nothing too formal about the introductions. Tilly simply rattled off their names as she pointed to each person, then she completed the formalities by adding, "And this is Jim, everyone." There were the initial hellos and almost immediately Steve and Andrew returned to their conversation on the best ever Crystal Palace football team line-up and Derek and Doris set off for a leisurely length or two of the pool. "Oh Jim, they all like you," Tilly beamed with that wonderful smile. "You are one of us now." Jim was a little confused as two had returned to their own conversation and two had swam off. Cath clarified it: "It's true, the boys wouldn't stop talking about bloody football for anybody you know."

Jim was sure that he had seen Cath before, but could not

put his finger on it, thinking of what to say Cath helped him to remember. "Last time I saw you in this pool you ducked me under and pinged my costume elastic, I want no repeat of that, Jim."

"You cheeky monkey, Jim, you need to behave yourself!" Tilly said with a poor attempt to look shocked.

"That was years ago, Cath, I was only about ten. I'm sorry, I will be better behaved, I promise."

"You better be, come on Tilly, let's go for a swim." Cath and Tilly swam off leaving Jim with Steve and Andrew who were still deep in debate over their Palace dream team.

Jim listened in on their conversation, having a soft spot for the local football team; he was interested in the selections they were putting forward. He heard many names mentioned, some he nodded to himself in agreement, to some he quietly shook his head, not wanting to interrupt. It was when Andrew put the player Alan Pardew forward as one of Palace's best midfielders that Jim could not keep his silence. "You have got to be joking, he was never a great player, I used to close my eyes when he got the ball. Mind you I could easily just blink as he never kept it for very long." Andrew looked up at Jim, "That's Al Al Super Al Super Alan Pardew' you're talking about." Steve interrupted, "Jim has got a point, he was no Lombardo, now that was a player, name one great thing Pardew did apart from stay on the bench."

"Score against Liverpool to win that FA Cup semi-final at Villa Park in 1990, what a day that was."

That was it. Steve, Andrew and Jim were locked in discussion about the merits of various players, the games they saw and the general highs and lows of following a team like Palace. Jim forgot he had just met this group of people, it felt very comfortable, he felt like he was part of the gang.

Tilly had long since returned from her swim and had to grab Jim's attention. "Come on Jim our time is up, it's nearly nine o'clock, they are going to start kicking us out soon." Jim had no idea where the time had gone and felt a little embarrassed he hadn't spent much time with Tilly. He didn't need to worry as Tilly looked pleased that Jim had obviously got on well with everyone. Tilly asked if Jim wanted to come back the next time the group met, the group fancied meeting again the next day as it happens, the answer was a definite yes: this was great.

Jim watched as Tilly left the pool. She was wearing a bright pink costume, almost as bright as her coat. He chuckled to himself, feeling quite contented, not realising he was the last one left in the pool. The attendant gave him a prod with one of those long sticks you find at the baths without saying anything and looking not too impressed, this must mean it was time to go. He had not expected the evening to be quite like that, but he was not disappointed, he was already looking forward to the next time – he might need to buy some new swimming trunks though.

5

Trouble at the pool

Saturday morning seemed very different for Jim. He had a warm feeling of contentment, which he didn't normally have. He had met a group of people and felt immediately like he belonged. This was the sort of thing Jim liked about being part of a strong community, something that seemed to be in decline and so should be valued and maybe fought for if necessary.

There was a spring in Jim's step as he took the familiar walk down Maple Road. Being a Saturday there was a different feel about the place, many of the people had more time on their hands, it being the weekend. Without fail there would be someone with a hangover from the previous night's drinking swearing that that was the last time they would have one of those kebabs, but they were determined to get up and try to walk it off, oh and tell everyone about it as if it was some sort of achievement.

"Jim, Jim, I had six pints last night and felt alright until I had that kebab," said a passer-by who obviously knew Jim. "I will be alright, just need a bit of fresh air." Fresh air, this was Penge. Jim just nodded. What did he want, a medal for his ability for drinking and kebab eating or sympathy for his self-inflicted heavy head? Never mind, he was harmless, Jim just kept walking.

There was a sports shop in the high street where Jim was

sure he could buy some new swimming trunks, he dare not wear those Wham ones again. Just a short walk and he was there, not a big shop but always seemed to have more inside than you expected, a sort of tardis.

Unfortunately for Jim this was Saturday and this meant the Saturday girl was looking after the shop. She was pleasant enough, just a little bit dim.

"Can I help you?" chirped the girl.

"Yes yes, I want to buy some swimming trunks," Jim answered.

"Are they for your son?" said the girl with an almost annoying higher-pitched chirp.

"No," replied Jim.

"For your grandson?" said the girl.

"They're for me," Jim was trying hard not to take offence. There was a short pause as the girl got used to the idea that someone like Jim would even consider going swimming before she eventually answered, "Bloody hell, I don't know quite what to suggest!"

Jim was finding it hard to hide his frustration. "I want to buy some swimming trunks, for me; this is a sports shop, I thought this might be the right place, or should I go to the newsagents next door?" The sarcastic comment was lost on the girl. "No they sell newspapers and stuff, we sell swimming trunks here. How about some like those?" The girl pointed to a display with a mannequin sporting a very brief pair of Speedos.

"You have got to be joking, they would do me an injury, not to mention get me arrested, what else have you got?" The girl looked Jim up and down.

"Yeah, you've got a point," then showed him where they had some other boxer type trunks. "We have these, but they're a bit boring."

"They're perfect," replied Jim. He found his size, even found a nice but not too over-the-top colour, paid the girl and left the shop as soon as he could. He was now ready for the pool on Tuesday. Equipped with his new trunks, he was looking forward to meeting the gang again, but most of all Tilly.

The pool seemed to be a little bit busier on Saturday, but still very quiet by the standards of the larger leisure pools in the surrounding area which most people preferred to go to. The same person was in the ticket office, this time she was painting her nails with the free sample she had got with her new magazine. "One adult please." No response from the ticket office.

"I said one adult please,"

"Oh my God I am rushed off my feet today."

"It doesn't look very busy to me," Jim replied, looking behind him; he could only see one boy behind him in the queue. The girl in the ticket office also saw the boy and seemed to be in horror, "Now there's a queue, I will never get to read about how to discover my perfect skin tone, mind you I am unlikely to see much sun in here, with this bleedin' queue." Jim eventually managed to pay for his ticket and make his way to the changing rooms. I suppose the ticket-buying process was all part of the charm of the place in some way.

Jim was feeling quite smart as he was about to enter the poolside. He had his nice sensible new trunks on and was looking forward to meeting his new friends. No sooner than he was by the pool he herd Tilly's voice, "Does this mean you are not a man anymore?" The whole pool looked round, but mind you that wasn't many people.

"You would have seen for yourself if I'd bought the speedos!" Jim replied. The people in the pool were not sure now where to look so eventually just carried on.

Jim got into the pool and made his way over to where the group were. "Hi Tilly, what a welcome, now it will get round Penge that I'm having a sex change!"

"Don't worry, the people in here don't care, anyway I can see that you're man enough Jim," Tilly replied with a cheeky grin. Jim was keen to learn more about the group and Tilly was happy to oblige. "Well there is Steve who works in an insurance office, Andrew who is a delivery driver, your typical 'white van man' I suppose, except his van is red! You have met Cath before it seems; she works at the betting shop in the high street, nobody dares to argue if they lose their bets. Cath is a bit of a tiger, isn't that right?"

"It's from the years I was with that dickhead Simon. I have tried anger management but the tutor wound me up too much."

"Never mind, it can be handy sometimes: the betting shop can't afford to employ a bouncer."

"Oh, and there is Derek and Doris; they used to have connections in show business but are pretty much retired now. They helped my son, Tom, to a career working with an agency. He is over in America now doing very well for himself."

Jim felt he knew a bit more about the group, also knew more about Tilly – Sharon mentioned she had a child. Not that this was a problem, it was just nice to know about it.

The main 'hot topic' of conversation today was the temporary closure of the big pool up at the Crystal Palace National Sports Centre, once the main sporting pool complex in the country with a teaching pool, a full fifty-metre pool and a diving pool with full range of diving boards. It would seem that it was in need of some essential maintenance and so had to close for the time being. "It's nice to see some investment in that place, about time too if you ask me," said Andrew. This seemed to be the general opinion: the sports centre with athletics stadium, pool complex and everything else had been slowly decaying and taken over by newer facilities over the county. Now that they had just had the London 2012 Olympic Games the new aquatics centre made Crystal Palace pool look very tatty and in need of a lot of work. Steve commented, "We might get a few more in here, at least it might keep this place going."

No sooner had Steve said that the pool seemed to gradually filling up: more people came in from the changing rooms. There were a few comments like "It's a bit small" or "Oh my God, I hope they reopen our pool soon."

"Well if they don't like it they know what they can do!" Cath said, maybe just a little too loudly.

"Come on, Cath, let's do a few lengths while there's still some room," Tilly diverted Cath's attention before she started a pool rage incident. Derek and Doris were still in the group, wearing their matching swimming caps. They looked right at Jim. Doris said, "Tilly likes you, doesn't she Derek?" nudging him in his ribs with her elbow.

"We can see that she has taken a shine to you, isn't that right, Derek?" This time Derek didn't need a nudge.

"You seem to have brought that smile back to her face; it's nice to see, there must be something special about you Jim."

"Come on, Derek, let's go for a swim, we don't want to embarrass him."

Jim was left in a sort of happy daze after Derek's

comment, is Tilly really interested in me? He could not help wondering what she saw in him, not that he minded, he quite liked the idea that they might take their relationship further. His mind was now racing with thoughts of what he should do about this, ask to take her to the pub again or perhaps push the boat out and go for a nice meal, go and see a show, or all three? Jim was so deep in thought that he did not realise that Steve and Andrew had been discussing the Crystal Palace home match against close rivals Charlton to be played that afternoon.

"What do you think, Jim – should they play three up front and give them a good battering? Jim? Jim? You're miles away. Do you think we should take 'em apart right from the start?"

"Sorry, Steve. Take who apart?" replied Jim in a rather startled manner. Andrew joined in, "Bloody Charlton that's who. I like it when we beat them, we better bloody beat them today I'm tellin' you." There was always an element of doubt with Crystal Palace, they should win this match but could also mess it up! This I suppose makes supporting a team like Palace a more interesting experience than one of those top teams that win all the time, where's the fun in that? The three of them then continued to debate and plan the downfall of poor old Charlton and how many Palace would win by. Steve had a season ticket so would be at the game and was getting more and more fired up. "We will be three up by half time," declared Steve, slapping his hands in the water. "For God's sake calm down; as long as we send them back beaten and knowing their place that's enough." Andrew just wanted to stop the splashing.

Suddenly there was a loud announcement over the tannoy. It was the voice of the girl from the ticket office. She seemed even more flustered than before. "Everybody has got ten minutes to leave the pool!" She must have forgotten to then turn the tannoy off because the whole pool could next hear, "What do you mean you booked the whole pool out for your group, we don't get bleedin' group bookings here!" then she addressed the pool again. "You have got five minutes now." It didn't seem to matter that it was only two minutes from the last announcement. The tannoy was still on: "Sodding synchronised swimmers, booking the poxy pool, this wasn't in my terms and conditions, I'll be asked to spin a fucking glitter ball next, oh bugger the bloody switch is stuck!" There was then a loud bang: the magazine must have been useful in turning the tannoy switch off.

By this time Derek, Doris, Cath and Tilly had re-joined the group and they were all looking at one another in disbelief at what was happening. Cath was the first to comment on this new situation, "You have got to be joking: kick us out of our pool, for what, synchronised swimming? This ain't happening."

Andrew added, "I've seen that synchronised swimming on TV. Pointless bloody rubbish and there will be sequins floating on a film of make-up grease in this pool by the time they are finished!" There was a nod of agreement in the group, this development was not a good thing, it used to be their pool, more or less, to be removed by something this ridiculous was a serious matter.

Before they knew it there were a group of girls in bright costumes covered in sequins and with overdone make-up entering the poolside from the changing room. Andrew was right about the mess they would make. The pool attendant was beginning to use his long pole to 'encourage' the last remaining swimmers to leave and make way for the 'sequined angels'. It was a bit like being rounded up!

"Prod me with that and my husband will shove it right up your arse!" The group turned and looked at Doris with an element of surprise but yet admiration. They had never heard Doris use that tone of voice before, but it showed the strength of feeling and fight they all shared over this situation.

Tilly gauged the situation pretty quickly. "Look we either take 'em on and fight them for the pool or leave and work out what's going on." Andrew and Cath looked as though the idea of fighting the invaders off there and then appealed to them, but no, beating up a bunch of schoolgirls was not the right way to go.

"Just one swing at that lanky one."

"No, Cath, that is not going to help."

"Come on, let's get out and see what we can do about this. Poor old Jim, just joined us and this happens," Tilly felt a mixture of sadness and anger at how this group of friends were being treated.

As Jim was climbing out of the pool a more mature voice from the 'invading group' cried out.

"Jim, is that you?"

Jim turned round and instantly recognised who it was. It was Julie, an old flame from long ago, before Jim married.

"What are you doing here?" Julie asked.

"I was having a sodding swim before this lot turned up!" Jim replied.

"These are my girls, Jim, aren't they beautiful? We have to use this old place while our pool is closed, it's a bit run down but it will just about do I suppose. We have the pool booked for our sole use, you don't mind do you?"

"Why would we all mind, Julie? Being kicked out for

this bunch. Why are they wearing lip gloss? It's bloody ridiculous!"

"Jim, they are sportswomen and have to look their best to perform; I am going to win the championships with these girls."

"That is just utterly ridiculous, this is not a sport and you can't just take the pool over."

"I can, Jim, my Stan has sorted it for me. Nice to see you again."

"Same old Julie, always get what you want, eh!" Julie just smiled as Jim left the poolside, but this was not finished, not by any means.

Jim knew that Stan was on the local council and would have arranged for Julie to have the pool because Julie always got her own way. No consideration to those using the pool, keeping Julie happy was far more important. This was not right, this was unjust; alright – if they want a fight they will get one!

6

Time for the battle plan

The group got changed and met afterwards in an area overlooking the pool where there were a few poorly stocked vending machines. OK if you want a can of sprite and a bag of beef and onion crisps, if that is not what you fancy, well never mind. Each of the friends were obviously still trying to take in what had just happened and were not best pleased about it.

"Who does she bloody think she is, barging in with those little tarts and kicking us out?"

"You can't call them tarts, Andrew, they are just schoolgirls," protested Cath.

"Yes, but from that local comprehensive school, Andrew may have a point," added Steve. Andrew turned to the window overlooking the pool.

"Look at that, it's pathetic, what is it meant to be?"

"Some think it's artistic don't they, Derek," added Doris.

"Yes dear, don't see it myself, there must be something better to do for a young girl around here these days." Derek was right, even if this was Penge.

Still pointing at the window, Steve demanded, "And who is that bloody woman?" Jim knew.

"That's Julie, she is used to getting her own way, always has been selfish, was a spoilt only child and a pain in the arse since."

"Do you know her, Jim?" asked Tilly.

"Yes, for a long time, we even went out together for a while; thank God she chose to marry Stan instead, that was a lucky escape.

"Who's this Stan then?" asked Steve.

"Used to be a good friend of mine; don't see him much now, he's either on council business or at his club, usually up to no good at either if you ask me!"

"Oh yes, I know him, runs the Penge Social Club. Been there a few times, God knows why. It's a bit of a dive."

"What do you mean a bit? The last time I was there I had warm gassy beer and some old bloke croaking his way through his unique version of 'My Way'. It certainly was his way, and to be frank, shit!"

"Thanks for that, Andrew, so nicely put," Tilly replied with an obvious sarcastic tone to her voice.

The group then started to share their experiences of Penge's 'premier night spot', the Penge Social Club. It was a typical, rather tired social club, caught in a bit of a time warp. As with similar establishments there was live music at the weekends, but to call it music may be being a bit generous: there was usually the typical club singer or a band of dubious quality managing to murder a selection of well-known tunes. This does not put off the regular clientele; no they love it, or at least they drink enough to convince themselves they love it. Every so often the act might not be too bad, but this only causes confusion – the regulars are not used to anything of quality, if they wanted that they would go somewhere else!

"When I was last there, there was a fight over a bar stool, it disrupted the music," Cath was only too happy to share the experience.

"Were the band distracted by it?" asked Doris.

"It was the band who were fighting, not enough stools for them all to sit down. When the band got up on the key change like bloody Westlife there was a fight to get a stool to sit back down on, bloody musical chairs. Mind you that was much better than their singing, we even called for an encore!"

"You must admit the place is a bit of a joke." Steve was right, none of the group would really want to go there after what they know of the place.

A thought came into Tilly's head. "What we need is someone to go and talk to this Stan bloke, what with being on the council and married to that woman, he might be able to do something about it. What do you think, Jim?"

"Well yes, perhaps, it could be worth a try," replied Jim.

"Good because that's what you are going to do. He's an old pal isn't he, we will all really appreciate it, Jim."

Jim looked around the group with their expectant faces. Tilly had one of her winning smiles, how could he say no? Knowing that backing out of this was not an option Jim asked, "I haven't seen Stan in years; I can't promise anything. Okay, when do you want me to go?"

Tilly was quick to reply, "Today, Jim, no time like the present, are we all agreed?" The group all thought this was a great idea; Jim felt a weight of expectation on his shoulders.

"We can meet up tonight for a drink and you can tell me how it went." Tilly then gave Jim her telephone number. "Give me a call later, Jim." Jim, right now, had mixed emotions. He was quite happy at getting Tilly's phone number, things appeared to be going quite well between them, but there was certainly more pressure to achieve something from his meeting with Stan because of this. This was certainly motivation to fight for the cause; you could be forgiven for thinking that Tilly was fully aware of this. Jim remembered hearing that they were holding auditions at the social club today for new acts to perform at 'Penge's premier music venue', he knew that Stan would probably be there. So it was straight to the club to see his old mate Stan.

The Penge Social Club was quite a large building at the end of the high street going towards Crystal Palace Park. From the outside it didn't look too bad in relation to the surrounding buildings, could do with a bit of work to brighten up the general appearance perhaps, it was only once you were inside the true character of the place was revealed. Once through the big heavy front door you were in a long entrance hall with a dark dirty patterned carpet and equally unappealing battered woodchip wallpaper, which appeared to have a range of colours – none of which represented the original colour from God knows how many years ago. There were old signed photographs on the wall of previous acts who had performed at the club – a wall of fame without so much of the fame if you like. The most famous you would recognise from the wall would probably be either Bobby Davro or The Krankies, what evenings they must have been!

Jim went straight to the bar at the front of the building, which seemed to have a few people waiting for their auditions. Some were warming up their vocal chords with a few exercises, others with a pint of warm, gassy beer. Jim asked the barmaid where Stan was. "If you are 'ere to audition you just wait your turn," was the swift reply.

"I don't actually want to audition, I can't sing, I just want to see Stan." Jim perhaps did not explain himself well enough as the barmaid replied, "Don't worry if you can't sing, not many here can if I'm honest, just give it your best and look confident luv." A few of the waiting auditionees heard the barmaid's comment and looked as if they were mildly offended, of course they thought they could sing. Jim tried again, "Look, I am not here to audition, I want to see Stan about something, he is an old mate of mine. Tell him it's Jim." The message seemed to get through this time. "Oh, okay, I'll go and tell him shall I?"

While Jim was waiting at the bar a quiet young man dressed as Elvis approached him. "Who are you going to be then?"

"Sorry, what do you mean?"

"Who are you going to be? You've got to be someone haven't you, you know like *Stars In Their Eyes*. Do you know, when I'm on that stage I even believe myself I am 'The King', it's an emotional experience." This slightly strange man then started to sing a few bars from what sounded a bit like 'Hound Dog' but it wasn't easy to be sure.

"Why don't you just be yourself?" Jim interrupted, more to stop the dodgy singing than anything else.

"Be myself? I'm a plumber, that's not what people want, that would never work!" He looked at Jim as if he must be mad. Thankfully, almost like an act of mercy, the barmaid reappeared and told Jim that Stan would see him. "He's down the hall in the back bar, but he says he's busy so be quick." Jim made his way towards the dark hall with the swirly carpet. Elvis was not pleased. "It's not his turn, I've been here for an hour, my sodding wig is starting to itch!" The barmaid was sympathetic: "Shut up and wait your turn."

As Jim was walking down the hall he passed what appeared to be one of his real musical heroes, he was sure that David Bowie had just left the audition room. Jim was stunned and could only muster a "Hello David" as they passed in the hall. David stopped, turned to Jim and gave him some advice, "If I were you I wouldn't bother, he's an idiot. I've played all over the world but not good enough for the Penge Social Club, eh!" David left muttering, "The bloke's a fool, why did I bother?"

Jim was still stunned: that was David Bowie, no doubt. He knew he had a house in Beckenham and had lived there for many years, when he wasn't in the USA. In fact Beckenham has a rich history of famous musical residents: Sparks, Haircut 100 and I lived in the same road as Kirsty McColl (some parts of this book are not fiction)! It turned out that the one and only David Bowie was back in the area and wanted to try some new material on a small stage with an intimate audience. The fact he had to first audition, and then get turned down, confirmed he had chosen the wrong venue.

Jim finally reached the back bar where he found Stan. "Jim, long time no see, what are you going to do, sing me a song!"

"I'm not here to sing, Stan, I just want a chat with an old mate."

"Thank God for that, you can't be worse than the last bloke, thought he was someone big, singing about Major Tom or something, bloody rubbish."

"That was David Bowie, Stan, he is a legend."

"No it wasn't, nothing like him, Beryl would have been dancing round her mop if we had someone that good in." They both turned to Beryl the cleaner and she didn't look like she had just been dancing round her mop. It was not worth the argument: that was David Bowie and clearly neither Stan nor Beryl were good judges of musical talent. "Now Jim, what do you want to talk to me about?" At that moment the next audition hopeful walked in, "Oh hang on Jim, let me just hear this bloke." It was the plumber, or should I say Elvis; he gave Jim an evil stare as he walked in, "Bloody queue jumper."

Stan called him to the stage. "Now who are you going to be?" There was a pause. "Ha, only joking with you, when you're ready." Next followed a more than painful rendition of 'Blue Suede Shoes' complete with slightly suspect pelvic movements which were making his wig slip. Stan turned to Jim, "Now this is more like it, look at Beryl." She was indeed dancing round her mop. "Yes mate, we like you, just right for the Penge Social Club, we will be in touch and book you in." Jim was stunned as the plumber left straightening his wig with a smug smile; he was truly terrible.

"OK Jim, tell me what's on your mind."

"Stan, it's about Julie, she seems to think she can kick me and my mates out of the local pool, can you have a word? I mean, it is not that fair on those who already use this pool is it?"

"Oh yes, the synchronised swimming club. I pulled a few strings and got my Julie the use of the pool, nothing too much for my Julie."

"Well the facility was pretty much empty and my Julie needed somewhere, what is the point of being on the council unless you can sort a few things out, eh Jim."

"That's not playing fair, Stan, many people enjoy their regular swim, it's an important part of their routine."

"Jim, the pool was never busy, just a few old fogies, no offence Jim. I've filled it with a wonderful local sports team. I've done the pool a great favour you know." Before Jim had a chance to protest the next auditionee walked in, a young girl who was quite nervous.

"Okay, luv, when you're ready, but hurry up I'm running behind." Stan did not put the girl at her ease. The girl however was quite good, she could actually sing. Jim was enjoying it until Stan barked, "Not what we're looking for luv," Beryl was not dancing round her mop at all. "Sorry luv, stick to singing to your hairbrush, you will get better." The girl left looking quite upset.

"Stan, she was good," Jim could not believe how she was treated.

"Jim, not good enough for my club, oh and I will let Julie have the pool if that's what she wants, I have passed a rule at council that sports clubs take priority, sorry about that."

Jim left feeling angry, Stan was bending the rules to keep Julie happy; he didn't care about those people just pushed aside, not the result he was hoping for. His parting words showed his frustration: "You're still a first class tit, Stan,"

Stan just smiled. "Nice to see you again, Jim."

The only positive was that his opinion of the entertainment standards of the Penge Social Club were confirmed. It was going to be difficult telling Tilly that he did not get very far with Stan, they were being pushed out and it was backed up by the local council.

7

Where there's a will, there's a way

Jim went straight back to his flat after his meeting with Stan, all the time thinking about how he was going to tell Tilly the bad news.

The mood seemed a bit down as he walked back up Maple Road. Crystal Palace could only manage a draw against Charlton, all the optimism of the morning was a distant memory. Jim walked past a man who was with his son and by the look of the faded face paint and long faces they had been to the game. The dad was trying to tell the boy that it didn't matter and that they would win next week, but it was obvious he was just as deflated.

Jim arrived back at his flat with Tilly's telephone number in his pocket – he had to phone her and break the news. He took a deep breath and went for it. "Hello Tilly, it's Jim."

"Jim, my little soldier, you've sorted it all out with your old mate Stan, I knew you could do it, the whole group will be so pleased."

"Not quite, Tilly." There was an uncomfortable pause, had Jim blown it?

"Jim, couldn't he talk some sense into her?"

"No, he bloody arranged it to keep her happy and made it official through the council." There was another pause, leaving Jim feeling helpless. "Well, we will see about that, meet me down the pub at eight o'clock. We need to find a way round this, see you later Jim."

"Oh okay, see you later." There was a strange sense of relief; we were going to fight this, yes, Julie and Stan had a fight on their hands, it was about time someone stood up against this sort of thing.

Before he knew it the time was 7.15pm. This was a sort of date, a date with a mission, Jim had to get ready. A quick wash, a clean shirt and, no, he was not wearing that terrible aftershave again. He took one last look at the bottle before it was thrown in the bin.

As he walked back down Maple Road there were the usual mix of people, some coming from the pub drowning their sorrows for the lack of a Palace win and some on the way to the pub dressed up for their weekend booze-up. This time Jim managed to walk past the kebab shop without being noticed; god that aftershave must have been strong. Jim was outside the pub at 7.55pm expecting to see the bright glow of Tilly walking down the road. Ten minutes passed and no sign of Tilly, until there was a voice behind him.

"Jim, there you are, I was waiting round the corner." It was Tilly, in a bright purple dress, how could he have not seen her there. "Jim, there's something different about you, you're not wearing that aftershave are you? Good thing too, I didn't like to say but it was a bit … er … you know."

Jim knew what she meant and could not help agreeing. "It's okay Tilly, I know it was rank. I've put it in the bin if that's a safe way to dispose of it, just don't tell my sister. I don't want to hurt her feelings. Shall we go in?"

The pub locals did not take much notice this time. Sure they realised that Jim was on a further date with Tilly, but like an episode of *Jeremy Kyle*, they had little interest unless there was going to be some sort of scene to entertain them. Jim asked Tilly what she wanted to drink. "Oh, just an orange juice and lemonade please, we've got business to discuss." Jim thought for a second he maybe should have the same but no, it was going to be a pint for Jim.

Once they had found a table Jim wanted to apologise for failing to get anywhere with Stan. Before he had a chance Tilly looked Jim in the eye and said: "I am so grateful to you for talking to that idiot Stan, we all knew we had no chance, it was a bit unfair to ask you really, but I thought it was worth a go, as you knew him and everything. I'm sorry." This was unexpected. Jim reached over to clutch Tilly's hand, in the process knocking the orange juice and lemonade across the table, the spill flowing towards Tilly like a tsunami. "Oh my God, I am so sorry." The locals began to take notice as this was more like what they had hoped for last time. Jim did not know what he should do, it did not seem appropriate to mop Tilly down with the cloth which had been passed to him to sort the table out. "Tilly I am really sorry, you can throw my beer over me if you like." The locals really had an interest now. "Go on luv, chuck it over him!" This situation had potential for them. To the disappointment of the crowd it wasn't as bad as Jim feared. "Jim, it's OK, you missed me, just about. I wouldn't mind another drink though, this time in the glass would be preferable." Tilly still had that wonderful smile; it looked like Jim had got away with it.

Once Jim had replaced the drink it was time to discuss what to do about being kicked out of the pool.

"Now tell me what this bloke Stan said."

"Well, he has passed some ruling at the council that only recognises that sports clubs can use the pool at certain times, just so that Julie can get her way with her synchronised swimming group. It's not even a bloody sport, bloody ridiculous."

"The bastard."

"Tilly."

"Sorry Jim it has to be said."

"Trouble is that Julie is used to getting what she wants."

"The bitch."

Jim just looked over at Tilly without protest, she had a point. "Well that's easy then, swimming is a sport, we are a swimming club aren't we? Next Tuesday we will go as usual and they can't kick us out."

"We will be the Penge Athletic Swimming Club, how about that?" Tilly had a good point, after all it was a council ruling that sports clubs had priority, so that was the way round it, even if they were not particularly 'athletic'.

They continued to discuss this plan and just chat in general until about 10pm when the noise in the pub just got a little too much to carry on their conversation without shouting to each other. Jim walked Tilly to her house, this time it seemed natural to hold her hand – there did not seem to be any resistance. When they reached the front gate they turned to each other and kissed – yes, a proper kiss. "I can get near you tonight Jim without being choked by your sister's aftershave."

"I promise I will not wear it again," replied Jim.

"I am not going to invite you in tonight Jim, don't get me wrong I like you, like you a lot, I just don't want to rush things." Jim understood; sure he fancied Tilly, but he was more than happy with how their relationship was going, why spoil things? He was just so happy to have found her, or at least his sister Sharon finally got it right.

"Right Jim, I will see you on Tuesday at the pool, ready for battle."

"I'll be there, we will show 'em, looking forward to it."

On the walk home Jim felt that warm feeling again but more intense. He was happy. Even though he had a fight on his hands which had made him angry he had not felt this happy in a long time. Jim slept well that night, he felt ready to 'boldly go where no man has gone before', and be the first to put Julie in her place, it would be about time. He had a newfound strength, something to fight for and someone to fight with. There was no way he was going to fail; he couldn't wait to get started.

Sunday mornings were usually very quiet down Maple Road, a bit like the calm after the storm with the evidence of the night before all around. There was all kinds of rubbish from fast food wrappers and beer cans to the odd half-eaten kebab – it would seem some could not face eating a whole one even when drunk! All of the people responsible for this would not be seen out and about until at least lunchtime, still sleeping off the effects of the night before. The only person Jim saw at 9am when he left his flat was the street cleaner who had the unpleasant job of clearing up the mess. The street cleaner was usually not that happy in his work but for some reason this morning was different. He was singing: "Oh what a beautiful morning, oh what a beautiful day," – this was quite odd but Jim could not help agreeing, Jim did have a wonderful feeling that everything was finally going his way. The cleaner's singing was briefly interrupted by "Jesus Christ, not another fucking kebab", then he carried on singing. "The sun has got his hat on…" There was indeed an unusual feeling of optimism in the air.

As Jim walked further down the road he reached the area where the market stalls sat. Yes there was more graffiti on Willie Plonker's sweet stall, something about what some lad had done with a bag of wine gums and a girl from the sandwich shop, I could not possibly repeat what it said as it may put you off wine gums. Jim kept walking, knowing William would be out later scrubbing this off but it was still far too early. This made Jim realise he was out earlier than usual. Even though he was on his way to Sharon's house it was too early to call, to kill a bit of time he would walk through the park, it was a nice morning for it.

It was quite a big park but it was nice to have a bit of green space locally to escape to sometimes. At first it appeared that Jim was the only person there but there was also a lone jogger, a young girl. As she jogged past she seemed to slip and over she went. "Are you alright, luv?" enquired Jim.

"Yes, I think so, just me being clumsy." The girl got up and brushed herself down. Jim recognised the girl, she was the one he had heard at the social club yesterday, the one who was actually good!

"Didn't I see you at that audition at the social club?"

"Er, yes, might have been, no use though, shouldn't have bothered for the response I got."

"Don't take any notice of Stan, he wouldn't know talent if it smacked him in the face, you were bloody good, anyone should have recognised that."

"Oh, thanks," the girl raised a smile. "Well nice to meet you." The girl waved and then continued her run. By this time it was late enough to call at Sharon's house, she would be up by now.

Sharon was up but still in her dressing gown by the time Jim got there. He was ushered in through the front door. "Jim come on in, you have a lot to tell me if the stories are true."

Jim knew that he was in for further interrogation. Jim was ready for it. "Shall I sit under big nose then?"

"Just sit down and shut up. Cup of tea?"

"Yes please."

Jim thought that might at least buy him some time to get comfortable, but no. Sharon cried out in the direction of the kitchen, "Jim wants a tea as well, Mum!" she then turned her attention to Jim. "I want to know if it's true."

"If what's true?"

Jim was trying his best to look like he had no idea what Sharon might be on about.

"Jim, is it true, have you… you know?"

"Have I what Sharon? Climbed a mountain; met the Queen; won the lottery, what do you bloody mean?"

Dot then walked in with the tea. "Did you shag her?"

"Mum, you can't ask 'im that… well, did you?"

Jim felt the two pairs of eyes bearing down on him demanding an answer. "If you mean Tilly I'm not saying."

Being evasive wasn't going to help. "Who else is there then? Bloody hell Mum, a couple of dates and he's gone sex mad and what's all this about a lottery win?"

"Calm down Sharon, we just kissed, there is no one else and I have not won the lottery."

"We know you kissed, you were seen, it's all round the town, but some reports have you going in for a bit more!"

"No Sharon, it was only a kiss, why spoil things by rushing in? I think we're getting on OK, I really like this girl."

"Just a kiss? I was told your tongue was halfway down her throat and your hand was somewhere else!"

"Mum, it was not like that, behave yourself," protested Jim.

Sharon and Dot seemed to eventually accept that there was little truth in the various rumours about Jim's night of passion; there is a way of thinking in Penge: 'Why let the truth get in the way of a good rumour' and if the rumour is good tell everyone.

"Well, anyway, you appear to be getting on okay; been a long time since you were so keen to go swimming, we want all the details Jim." Sharon was determined to know.

"It's going alright, things are going well. Sorry I can't tell you anything more juicy, but we have been kicked out of the pool though."

At this point John walked in, he was only half awake. "Kicked out the pool? So those rumours are true about skinny dipping with your new girlfriend!"

"No, bloody hell; we have been kicked out by a bunch of synchronised swimmers," protested Jim. There was a brief pause then all but Jim burst out laughing.

"That's better than all the other rumours put together. Sorry, Jim, wait until the girls 'ear this." Sharon was less than sympathetic.

"I'm not giving up though; they're in for a fight I'm telling you."

"Of course, Jim, she will like to see some fight in you… in the meantime you can put those shelves up for me. Kicked out by synchronised swimmers, you're having a laugh," Sharon pointed to the corner of the room where the shelves and his tools were waiting. "Come on let's leave him to it."

"Yes he could do with a good screw," added Dot. This sent John into another burst of laughter. "Gran, you're the best."

"She didn't mean like that," protested Jim, but it was likely that she did.

8

The opening shots

Tuesday came round quickly and Jim was looking forward to going to the swimming that evening. It wasn't just meeting Tilly again, he could not wait to take the fight forward. He was certainly a man on a mission.

Jim left his flat in good time. It was arranged that the group would meet outside the pool at 7pm and go in together, they were after all a sporting club and they needed to show that. It had started to rain so there weren't many people along Maple Road but still enough to ensure that there would be a few comments sent in Jim's direction. It could not be disguised that Jim was carrying an old-fashioned type duffle bag, the sort we used to carry our swimming things in when we were kids. Jim was indeed carrying his swimming trunks and towel in this bag which was just giving ammunition to those wanting to voice their words of wisdom.

"Hey Jim, kicked out by a bunch of girls?" or "I don't think you can join their club mate, there's a law against that sort of thing." Of course Jim's love life was also fair game. "Remember mate there's no petting and ripping her costume off is definitely not allowed in the pool!"

Not everybody knew enough detail to make an informed comment but that was no reason to stop them. "Going dancing again Jim, not with your two left feet … and they're not any bleedin' good!" This was usually followed by a loud laugh, but not from Jim, he would just smile and walk on like always. It was still a comfort that they cared enough to give him abuse. The debate between the hecklers he left behind however was often funny. “He’s not going dancing Alf you great tit, it’s some sort of swimming thing, what are you on about?”

“Who are you calling a tit you great arse?” etc. etc.

It didn’t take long before Jim reached the pool, ready to join the rest of the group in a show of solidarity. Steve, Andrew, Cath, Derek, Doris and of course Tilly were already there waiting. “Here he is”, “Ready for the fight” and “We will bloody show them” welcomed him to the group. “If I see that cow, whatever her name is, I am going to drag her in the pool and duck her under.”

“Cath, for God’s sake calm down. Julie will not be here again today, didn’t you go to your anger management class?”

“I did, that’s why I’m angry.”

Jim saw no reason why they couldn’t have their swim as normal, and make a point that they can’t just kick them out.

“Well, Jim, look over there then.” Andrew pointed to a group approaching the pool entrance. It was Julie with some of her synchronised swimming team.

“That’s it. I’m going to kill the bitch.”

“Cath, calm down.” Tilly managed to stop Cath making a physical attack. Instead they all glared as Julie and her girls walked past.

This did not seem to have much of an effect on Julie. “Hello Jim, nice to see you again with your friends, sorry you couldn’t go in, but my girls come first, need to keep the training going if we’re going to win.”

“What do you mean can’t go in; we haven’t tried yet, we’re going in, it’s a sodding public pool, Julie.” Jim remembered what Stan had said about priority for sporting clubs. "We are a swimming club, a sporting swimming club, just as much right to the pool as you have even under your Stan's new rule."

"Really? Good luck with that Jim." Julie smirked as she led her girls through the entrance.

"Well, what are we waiting for?" said Andrew. "Let's get in there and this time kick those little slappers out before they create a glittered oil slick." Rather than someone tell Andrew off for his disrespectful language they all agreed and made their way in.

Manning the ticket office was the same useless girl Jim saw on his first visit, she was reading a different magazine though. Tilly thought that she would take the lead and approached the old-fashioned window to the ticket office.

"Excuse me … excuse me?" There was no response; she had to grab her attention somehow. "Look there's a mouse!" At that point the girl leapt up with a scream, launching her magazine into the air.

"Fucking hell! Where is it? Don't let it near me!" Tilly's trick had worked. "Now I've got your attention we would like to buy our tickets to go in."

"What, for a swim? Where's that sodding mouse?"

"Of course we want a swim, and there's no bloody mouse."

The girl looked puzzled. "Why did you say there was a mouse?"

"To get your bloody attention. Now, can we buy our tickets?" replied Tilly.

The girl looked disgusted at being tricked, and being disturbed from the latest celeb sex scandal she was reading about. "You bitch. I was really busy and you interrupt me with some fucking invisible mouse!"

"Mind your language young lady." Derek was obviously not too impressed with the ticket girl's outburst.

"What's it to you, and who are you calling a fucking lady?" This ticket girl was the sort of Penge girl you wouldn't want to take home to meet your mother.

"Is there any chance we can buy our tickets now?"

Cath was beginning to lose patience with this situation. The ticket girl looked her in the eye and with an almost expected lack of charm answered, "You ain't coming in; the pool's reserved for sports clubs or something like that, it's this new rule doing my bloody head in. It's only when that bloody woman turns up, then it's only sports clubs!" So it would seem that every time Julie turned up with her synchronised swimmers she would have the run of the pool, Stan had organised that alright.

Jim was ready for this. "We are a sports club, a swimming club, so now you can let us in can't you." The girl now looked puzzled. "You lot a sports club? But you're just a bunch of old people, you're all past it. Oh and you're not bloody going in!"

Cath was by this time getting rather angry. "I'll show you who's past it you little tramp."

Tilly had to hold Cath back from battering the ticket office window. The girl reacted by telling the group that they risked being barred for aggressive behaviour and that they should go to the old people's meeting house to calm down with a nice cup of tea. This was not perhaps what they wanted to hear.

Jim could sense the anger within the group growing and lynching this useless girl may not help them, they may not get in today but had to still find a way to fight this, without being arrested for GBH. "I think we should go now before we do something we may regret."

"Jim's right." Tilly could see this was the right thing to do. "Let's leave this idiot to her magazine." There was the exchange of looks confirming that this was far from over.

As they were about to leave one of the girls from the synchronised swimming team burst out from the changing room looking like she was in tears. Jim recognised her, it was the girl he saw at the audition and later jogging in the park. "Are you alright luv?"

She turned to Jim and did her best to put on a brave face. "Oh it's you, hello, I'm okay."

Jim could see things were not at all OK and asked again, "Come on, what's wrong?" At this point she burst into tears and fell into Jim's arms, which took everyone by surprise, most of all Jim. The group of friends turned to one another to see if anyone knew who this girl was. His daughter? Might be. His young girlfriend? Can't be. Andrew gave Steve a little knowing nod as if to say 'well done Jim, didn't know you had it in you'. Tilly turned to Cath as if to ask 'is Jim two-timing me for someone far younger than me?' Derek and Doris just looked a little bit confused.

Jim comforted the girl but thought he should do something more. "Would it help if you told me about it, do you want to go for a drink or something?" The girl looked up, had a think and then to everyone's surprise, agreed. "Yes, alright, I could do with a drink right now." She must have been close to eighteen so he supposed this would be okay. Jim still did not know the girl's name. "I'm sorry luv, I don't know your name."

"It's Darcy," replied the girl.

"That's a nice name. I'm Jim."

"I'm bloody going with you." Tilly wanted to know what the hell was going on. Jim and Tilly left the group making sure that they would all meet again at the pool next time, there was no giving up, then they went with Darcy to the pub just down the road from the pool.

Once they were in the pub and seated with their drinks Jim could see that Tilly wanted to know who this girl was, and that he should explain and quickly. "Tilly, this is Darcy. I saw her at the auditions at Stan's club, she was the only one there who could actually sing yet she was told she was no good. She looked today just like she looked leaving that audition, something is not right here, I feel like I should help."

Tilly was still not sure what was going on. "But why should you help her? Sorry no offence luv, but you don't even know this girl."

Darcy looked a little uncomfortable. "I should go, I don't want to be a problem."

"No, please stay. I got an idea how you were treated at the social club and I see something similar has just happened, we should have a chat I suppose."

"Oh okay, if you're sure."

"Just sit down and tell us, whatever your name is."

"I'm Darcy."

"Well I'm Tilly and I can see you have met Jim; let's hear about it if it will help."

The regulars in the pub by this time were almost falling off their bar stools trying to listen in on the conversation.

"I've been told that I am not good enough for the synchronised swimming team – after I have put together all the routines, this is the thanks I get."

"Who said you weren't good enough?" Jim asked.

"It was Julie. Sorry, it's the leader of the team, she's Julie."

"I know Julie, she is married to Stan, the idiot at the club who said you couldn't sing."

"It's because I'm better than Julie's daughter; she has got the routines from me but does not want me to outshine her daughter in the team."

"Oh I see, the bitch!" Tilly was outraged at this further example of Julie's behaviour. There were a few approving nods around the pub as well, Julie was getting to be well known for being a first-class bitch.

Jim, in an effort to show support told Darcy how he would love to see Julie taken down a peg or two, somebody needed to beat her. Tilly had a moment of inspiration. "We will beat her, and at her own game."

"What do you mean; how?" Jim looked puzzled.

"With Darcy's help we start our own synchronised swimming club with our group, get in that pool and give her a run for her money. Darcy are you in?" Darcy was surprised by the suggestion. She had seen the group, but why not give it a go, it was a little bonkers but it might work. At the very least it would disrupt what Julie was doing.

"Yes, alright, count me in."

"Are you both completely mad!" Jim could not believe what he was hearing. The response was that maybe they were, but why not try, what was there to lose? It was a choice of being beaten by Julie and her girls now or going down with a fight possibly losing all dignity in the process. "Ok, let's give her something to think about. I'll do it."

And so in that moment Penge's newest synchronised swimming club was formed, they may not be what you would imagine such a club to be but their performance will certainly be one to remember!

9

We're a sports club!

The next morning Jim was at Sharon's house, all part of the normal routine. Before Jim started to investigate the dripping tap in the bathroom he was given a cup of tea. They were sitting in the kitchen, not under 'the nose of Manilow' thank God. Jim felt he had to tell Sharon about the latest 'pool wars' development.

"We've started a synchronised swimming club."

Sharon looked at him and with the corners of her mouth starting to rise, just checked if she heard correctly: "Did you say a synchronised swimming team?"

"That's right."

There was a pause and then Sharon burst into fits of laughter. "You and your pals doing that pool dancing load of cobblers," she was still full of laughter, "this I have got to see!"

"What's so funny – if they can do it so can we. If that what it takes to get in and use our pool."

"But Jim, you're a bunch of old farts and know nothing about how to do it, it will be funny to watch you though – careful you don't drown!"

Dot had overheard the conversation and while maintaining a straight face, walked into the kitchen. "It's lovely that you have an interest to follow with your new friends, of course there is no danger of looking like a complete tit is there? Are you going to wear one of those sparkly costumes and buy your own make-up? What a picture. Sharon you need to be careful, he will be going through your wardrobe next and calling himself Mary. You've always been a strange boy Jim."

"It will be OK; we have Darcy from Julie's club to show us all the moves." Sharon had received reports of Jim and Tilly having a drink with a mystery girl; the general thought was that they were having a threesome; this girl must be Darcy.

"I bet she is showing you some moves; does Tilly mind or does she join in?"

"For pity's sake, Sharon. Darcy has just been kicked out of Julie's group and was probably the best one there, she also knows all the routines, she is going to help us get going."

"I bet she will get you going." Dot perhaps did not mean the routines Jim was talking about.

As Jim was left to fix the dripping tap he could still hear Sharon and Dot laughing at the prospect of Penge's newest sporting great. He took no notice, he was determined to do this no matter what they thought about it, the trouble would be convincing the rest of the group what a great idea this was.

When the group had a meeting later that day the initial reaction was not great.

"Have you lost your marbles? Us doing that rubbish. Have you had a look around? We're not exactly built for it are we? I know for a fact that my husband is not a young slim girl, you're not are you Derek?" The group had met at the pub so that Jim, Tilly and Darcy could share the plans they had to continue their fight. It is rare that anyone heard Doris speak up in that way and it came as quite a surprise, there was, however, general agreement that this was quite a ridiculous idea.

"You expect us to do all that bloody water dancing, you must be barking mad."

"Quite possibly Andrew, but it's a way to get back into our pool; we need to show them we are not easily beaten." Jim was not going to find it easy to convince them.

"Have you forgotten one little detail? We do not have a clue how to do this rubbish," Cath added. "It's not as if we are going to get any help from one of those little tarts are we?" This was an unfortunate prompt for Tilly to introduce Darcy.

"Everyone, this is Darcy. She has joined us from the synchronised swimming club and is going to show us what to do." There was a brief uncomfortable silence before Darcy was quite rightly welcomed to the group.

"I am sure that you are not all tarts." Cath seemed to want to dig a bigger hole for herself. Darcy gave a rather nervous smile and fortunately did not make a run for the door.

Andrew wanted to know why Darcy had left her club so she explained how she was so badly treated and how they would probably miss her, this seemed to relax the initial tension of the situation and bring her into the group. They had a common goal: to get back into that pool and to show Julie she had a fight on her hands – she was not going to have it her own way this time.

"So you know how to do this stuff then?"

"Andrew, she was the best they had and that was why Julie didn't like it – a threat to that precious little daughter of hers." Jim was now definitely behind the idea and having Darcy to help them.

"The stuck up little slapper!" Everybody seemed to agree

with the opinion Cath had about Julie's daughter.

"But do you really think we could do this? I know we need to get back in our pool and all that but Andrew is right, look at us." Darcy looked slowly round the group and then turned back to Steve who asked the question. She drew upon the motivation course that she had just attended at work, took a deep breath and told the group how it was going to be.

"We all have an inner strength, we just need to release it. There are no limits to our potential, believe in—"

"Oh for God's sake this is just a load of talk."

"Let her finish, Steve." Tilly gave Steve a look to give the clear message that no more interruptions were welcome.

"As I was trying to say, there is no reason why we can't try. I know the routines and you can all swim can't you?" What I mean is let's show them that you're not all past it, we will show them what we can do and get you back into that pool."

"Past it; neither me or my husband are bloody past it, isn't that right, Derek?" But that was it, none of the group felt like they were past it or over the hill, and if that's what people were thinking then perhaps they should show them what they could do. You could be sure that Julie and her group of girls would think that, after all they had already kicked them out of the pool, they would never expect them to come back with a better routine!

"You know what? You're right. Let's do it, let's show them."

There were nods and punches in the air as they all agreed with Andrew. That was the moment they all realised that this is what they had to do; they were not past it, no way, and they were going to show it. The next time they went to the pool they would be a synchronised swimming club and have as much right to use the pool as Julie had.

It seemed a long time to Friday. There were unusual sightings of various members of the group jogging around the streets or park to get some sort of fitness, well I say jogging but it was more like a painful stagger. The levels of fitness were not currently very good. There were also a number of enquiries to join the local gym, even the introductory sessions were leaving their scars on the unconditioned (but not past it) bodies. By the time Friday came they were all aching in places they didn't know could ache.

As arranged they all met outside the pool on Friday evening. Jim was a little startled to also see Sharon, Dot and John turn up. "Sharon what are you doing here?"

"Hiya Jim; we wouldn't miss this for the world. Come on let's go up to the spectators' gallery with a pack of crisps!" There was the look of expectation on their faces, this was going to be worth missing *Eastenders* for.

Once all the group had arrived they went in and approached the ticket office. It was the same useless girl behind the counter, when she bothered to look up from her mobile phone she recognised the group immediately.

"Not you lot again, bloody mouse and all that. Why don't you bugger off, you're not coming in, it's sports clubs only, not stupid old people!" The group were not put off by this, a little annoyed maybe but not put off. Tilly thought it best that she approached the girl as the others looked like intent on wringing her neck.

"Hello, sorry about the mouse and all that. You can let us in because we are now a synchronised swimming club." The girl looked a little confused.

"You lot doing that, you can't be serious, you don't have the first idea what to do. Anyway there is a club already in doing it!" Tilly called Darcy forward.

"This is our coach and if they can get in so can we, I am sure the pool is big enough for us too." The girl was still not sure. "I was told to only let the synchronised swimming club in."

"And now there's another one, so let us in or speak to her." Tilly smiled as she pointed to Cath. Cath had that look on her face, she was ready for a fight. There was a look of fear in the girl's eyes.

"Oh go bloody in then see if I care, anyway you will be crap, don't drown yourselves now." They all paid for their tickets and went past the ticket office to the changing rooms. They were in: this plan was beginning to work.

Once changed they entered the pool to find that Julie's group were already in and about to start their practice session. There was a loud cheer followed by a sarcastic laugh from the viewing gallery when Jim walked in. Julie looked a little confused at what was going on. "Jim, nice to see you again but what are you all doing here? The pool is only for my girls tonight, you need to leave I'm afraid."

"Julie, we are now a synchronised swimming club just like you."

There was a loud giggle from Julie's girls.

"Well maybe not quite like your lot, but we're a club and staying for our session."

"But Jim, you can't be serious, you have no idea what to do."

At this point Darcy walked in.

"She is going to show us."

Julie looked at Darcy and did not look very pleased.

"You traitor, you're going to teach this lot, are you serious? Look at them!"

Darcy drew on her inner strength (probably from one of the courses at work), and replied: "Julie, I don't care, I'm with them now, at least they want me." There was a further giggle from the girls.

"Darcy, it's OK, you can come back if it means that much to you." There was a pause while they all looked to Darcy, sort of expecting her to go back to Julie as if the previous bad treatment hadn't happened.

"Piss off, Julie. Right, come on group, let's get started." There was a cheer and a ripple of applause from the balcony.

As you would expect the first session was a bit of a disaster. Darcy was doing her best to keep it as simple as possible but it was truly terrible. This was good news for the balcony, this was what they had come to see and they were loving it. There was still tension between the two groups, at one stage one of Julie's girls got a little too close to Cath and she grabbed the elastic from her goggles, letting it snap into the back of her head. Steve saw this and went to reach for another of the girl's costumes to ping the strap. Tilly saw this in time and let him know that getting arrested would not really help them. Darcy was finding it difficult to get the group to focus but little by little they began to get the hang of a few very simple moves, sometimes in time with one another. There was, however, no doubt that this was not going to be easy.

The balcony were still enjoying the entertainment, cheering at every unplanned slip and splash. Sharon and Dot continued to be quite vocal, but John had gone very quiet, he was looking at Darcy. John could not look away from Darcy, he was quite taken by her, what a girl! Those in the pool were fully aware of the 'appreciation' they were getting from the balcony and at one point Darcy looked up to where the noise was coming from. Darcy saw John looking at her, something must have clicked (at this point you, as the reader, might want to play some romantic music), Darcy smiled, John smiled back; could this be young love in Penge? Darcy had to break away from John's gaze as Derek and Doris were getting in a tangle and Cath was about to attack another of the girls, but the smile on her face remained and perhaps a bit of a blush.

The session continued in much the same fashion with Julie casting half an eye on what Jim's group was doing. She could see that they were, to be honest, still hopeless. Julie was not going to make any allowances due to this being the first training session. "Girls, girls, stop for a minute now. Just have a look at that lot and see how bad they are – remember girls that they will never be anywhere as good as you are. Sorry, Darcy, but we won't miss you at all." There was a supportive giggle directed across the pool. Darcy and the group heard this but dug deep to keep their composure. To lose their tempers would be a bad move. The best way to fight them would be to carry on and not give up. Julie could sense that she was being ignored and decided to end her practice a bit early, giving Darcy in particular a sarcastic glare as they left the pool. The gallery were not so quiet letting Julie know exactly where she should go, a bit like booing the pantomime villain. That was it: they had won the first battle. They had seen them out of the pool. It was a moment to celebrate. None of the group thought it would be so easy to see them off.

"That's it, we've won, we can stop all this now."

Andrew was so wrong, they had won the battle but the war was about to begin and Darcy knew it. "We have a long way to go and the session is not over." Darcy was going to keep them working, she knew Julie would be back.

The next morning Jim was still on a high, he was almost skipping down Maple Road on his way to Sharon's, even though he was feeling a bit stiff from the training in the pool. The news was out about his participation in the synchronised swimming (Sharon was not good at keeping things to herself and word can spread very rapidly in Penge). There were a few knowing looks in Jim's direction and, of course, always someone prepared to add their comments. "Go on, give us a twirl, don't be shy" or "Ballet in a swimming pool now that's a man's sport. I play rugby, I must be a fucking poofter". Of course Jim was used to this sort of thing and to be honest hardly noticed, he just directed a polite nod and a 'good morning'. Willy Plonker was cleaning up his stall as he saw Jim walk down the road.

"Hey Jim do you want some bonbons, something to give to those girls you are eyeing up?" This was followed by a rather nasty sneering look. Jim did not take up the offer of the free sweets.

It wasn't long before he was at Sharon's door. Before he had a chance to knock the door was opened before him. "Mum get the kettle on, our hero is here. Jim go in the kitchen you daft bugger." There was a full reception in the kitchen, both Dot and John were waiting for him.

"That was bloody hilarious Jim. You lot looked totally useless but it was worth missing the telly for. My mates from the bingo want to go next time they could do with a laugh."

"Thanks Sharon. I'm pleased we provided you with some entertainment but we did see them out of the pool, we saw Julie and her lot out of the pool."

"Oh that, her lot were much better than you but yes you seemed to rattle her, seeing her leave with that look on her face made it even better."

"She had it coming, always spoilt that one." Dot had known Julie from when she was young and knew what she was like.

"Well Mum we will keep coming back and we will show her, we will get better with Darcy's help." Sharon and Dot still found this to be a great joke but did deep down feel quite proud of what Jim was doing.

John was keeping very quiet but at the mention of Darcy's name he spoke as if in a trance. "She's beautiful." There was a short quiet pause on hearing this.

"Oh my God, my boy is in love, I do believe he is actually in bloody love."

"She's lovely."

"About time he took a girl out, not good for a boy to be stuck up in his room playing with himself!"

"Mum, stop, I think it's sweet, his Uncle Jim will have to introduce them, won't you Jim."

"She looked at me and smiled, she's beautiful."

"Jim listen to him, isn't it sweet? Has she got a boyfriend? She's not gay is she, not got any kids has she?"

"Don't start, Sharon, I don't know, she's just helping us out, I don't know her life history!"

"Well you can find out can't you and then set up a meeting for them. My boy in love with an actual swimmer, who would have thought it." When Sharon had her mind made up she was going to match make, there was little point in arguing, as Jim knew only too well. John was still in a bit of a dazed state and Sharon's plans seemed to just go over his head.

"John, do you want to meet Darcy, if you do why not come down on Tuesday night, only if you want to there's no pressure." Sharon was intent on taking charge of the situation. "We're all coming down Jim and the bingo girls if they want to come. Don't worry John you won't know we're there at all." This was hardly going to be the case. Jim knew that he would have to protect John from Sharon's interference, meeting Darcy should not be a spectator event.

10

They're no match for us

Tuesday evening had arrived and following their success in seeing Julie's group out of the pool, Jim, Tilly and the rest were there early. They had managed to get past the ticket girl who by now had admitted defeat, it was too much like hard work to continue to fight their entry. The 'fan club' had also arrived. Sharon was true to her word and the balcony was full of her friends from the bingo, together with Dot and John. They were all eagerly awaiting the entertainment to come together with watching a potential romance develop. John was, however, feeling a mixture of excitement at seeing Darcy again coupled with being nervous at being put in the spotlight – Sharon did not mean to put pressure on him, but there was. There was a loud cheer as they made their way out of their respective changing rooms; this came as a bit of a surprise for our sporting heroes but it gave them a sense of pride. There were a few nudges in the balcony when Darcy appeared together with knowing looks in John's direction. Jim looked up at John as if to tell him not to worry, it will be OK.

They were all in the pool with Darcy ready to start the training session when Julie and her group began to arrive. It would have been quite wrong to assume they had seen them off for good. Before they dived in Julie called them together.

"Look girls, take a look at them; this is the pathetic sight of those who have no idea what they are doing, they will never be as good as you – in fact I don't know why they are in our pool!" This little speech was made audible to the whole pool, quite on purpose. There were boos from the balcony: it was the pantomime villain who had just walked in, they were enjoying the show. Our heroes on the other hand were not so happy.

"What does she mean their pool, bollocks to that I'm going to hit her."

Tilly managed to keep Cath from committing assault and called the group together for their own team talk. "Look, we may not be able to do this very well, but don't forget we're back in here."

Darcy interrupted Tilly, "Wait, wait a minute, they're not as good as Julie thinks they are, the only person with any clue about doing a decent routine is, well, me and I'm with you now. I can make you better than them."

There were some disbelieving laughs from the group, Darcy put a stop to them. "We want to show that lot don't we, well we are going to enter the competition they are working towards, and beat them!" The balcony was lapping this up with a few cries of "Fight! Fight! Fight!"

There was a pause and then Jim felt he had to comment on what Darcy had just said.

"Are you off your bloody rocker? No offence, we really appreciate you helping us get back in the pool but honestly, just look at us, we are not exactly built for this, none of us are sporting young girls any more, some of us never have been!" There were a few agreeing nods within the group; starting this synchronised swimming thing was one thing, they were back in the pool despite Julie's efforts but beat them in an actual competition, not likely. Darcy was very serious about this. She had helped the group achieve their goal of overcoming Julie's block on their pool use but her goal of beating Julie in competition remained.

"For this competition there is nothing in the rules about being a young girl, trust me I have checked." Some of the group looked down, wondering what exactly she had checked. "I'm telling you that bunch of tarts are not that good and we will be able to beat them."

"I told you they were tarts," protested Andrew. Darcy was not prepared to accept any resistance and the group, in an act of solidarity, were not going to show weakness, they had to give this a go.

So Darcy had some fancy moves to teach them, well why not? She clearly had a point to prove and they were fighting a common enemy. The balcony was really getting excited at the prospect of the situation escalating into mild violence and they were shouting out as if they were on a *Jerry Springer* show. They were quite disappointed when both groups just stayed in their own halves of the pool and continued with their sessions. Darcy knew she had to continue at a fairly basic level so got the group doing some basic exercises. There were a few groans as the joints were being extended in ways they had not been for a long time. This was harder work however than the first session they had. It only took a few minutes of this before the first signs of dissent started to show.

"Bloody hell this is starting to hurt!"

"Shut up and keep going, this is just the warm-up," Darcy was not going to let them slack. There were a few despairing looks around the group. The balcony viewers began to get a bit bored with this and decided to leave. There were a few parting cries of "Go on you can take them" or just "Hit that blond tart on the left". Sharon shouted out to Jim, "We're off now. I will leave John with you." John was not ready to leave, he could not take his eyes off Darcy.

Despite the lack of fitness and flexibility which was quite obvious, Darcy did manage to work the group on a few basic moves. OK it was going to be a challenge, they were hopeless and at times looked like on the point of drowning, but slowly they began to get the hang of what Darcy had shown them. Make no mistake though there was a long way to go. They would bump into each other, splash when they shouldn't splash and choke from intake of pool water, but they kept going. They did spins, twirls, dives and all sorts, sometimes looking almost in time. After what seemed like an eternity of pain, Darcy called an end to the session, the group could hardly manage to drag themselves out of the pool. Julie's group finished soon after and still looked full of energy as they skipped past them on the way to the changing room, with a few sarcastic looks and giggles thrown in. It was a good job that Cath was knackered otherwise the blonde girl would have been thrown in.

John was waiting in the ticket area for Jim and didn't have to wait too long. "Ok John, what do you think? I felt like a bit of an idiot to be honest."

"She's great."

"Who do you mean, John?"

"Your coach, she's great."

"Oh you mean Darcy. Yes she certainly got us working, we are all feeling a bit knackered."

"She's amazing."

Jim could see that John was probably more interested in Darcy rather than her coaching abilities. It was clear to Jim that he should arrange for John to meet Darcy. It was better for John that he did something before Sharon decided to take over the arrangements.

"John, I don't want to put any pressure on you, but do you want to meet Darcy?"

"Eh, who is Darcy?"

"The girl you can't get out of your head you twit, do you want to meet her?"

"Err yes, I suppose." John looked a little embarrassed and a little red in the face but yes he wanted to meet her.

"Well that's good, John, because here she is." Darcy just happened to be walking past at that moment. "Darcy, there is someone I want you to meet." So much for no pressure.

"Hi Jim, did you like that session? We will give them a surprise or two yet trust me." Her eyes then turned to John.

"Darcy this is John, he likes your… err… coaching technique."

She smiled, "Do you now, do you want to join in the next session then?" John was a bit stuck for words.

"Err no you're alright, I mean it's great but err, I can't swim."

"He can swim he is just a bit shy, Darcy." Jim gave John a pat on the back. Darcy smiled again, "Well I guess I will see you again then John, as for you Jim it will be back in the pool for more hard work, bye then." Everyone else had left by this time so it was time for Jim to walk home with John.

"She's so amazing." John still appeared to be in a daze.

Jim smiled back at him, "Why did you say you couldn't swim you berk, come on, time to go home."

Once they were back at Sharon's it was all quite low key, it was a good thing that she had not fully noticed John's appreciation of Darcy. OK she was aware that John fancied the girl but right now she was more concerned with the lack of an all-out fist fight in the pool. "You should have laid into them Jim, jumped up little twits, who do they think they are, as for that Julie she has it coming to her that one."

"However tempting, we can't beat them up Sharon, that just would not be right."

"That's a pity. I must say you did look a sight, that girl seems to have some faith in you though."

Jim smiled, "She's OK, we might even get the hang of this with her help."

Sharon laughed, "In your dreams Jim. I suppose you would like a cup of tea, I might even find a bit of cake if John hasn't eaten it all, you must have an appetite after all that water dancing stuff." Jim had a little smile to himself; maybe they could dream, what if they could get the hang of it, that might just surprise a few people. As for John, Jim was happy that Sharon seemed more interested in thumping Julie than organising her son's love life, for now at least.

11

The hard work has just started

Jim woke up on Wednesday morning with pain in muscles he forgot existed. It felt like a major exercise to even get out of bed. Even though there was nobody to hear him he still groaned as if to invite sympathy from somewhere. It was no good, he had to get himself going, maybe his routine morning walk would help loosen things up and ease the pain. Things were not looking promising as he struggled to get to his front door, using the wall or anything fixed down for support.

Once outside Jim had to take tentative steps as anything more resulted in sharp pain, the result was a sort of shuffle, a bit like a floundering penguin. The people who were out and about were quick to notice. "Are you alright Jim, what have you done to yourself?" Jim tried to raise a smile and walk normally as if nothing was wrong. This was a big mistake as it only resulted in Jim crying out as the pain hit him and slowing almost to a standstill. Those who had previously enquired about his health would just then move on, "Don't lay it on now, what do you want, sympathy?" Well what did he expect from the population of Penge. There were, of course, some who were not so kind and all sorts of remarks were sent in Jim's direction. "Come on Jim, hurry up they say it's going to rain tonight, you don't want to be caught out in that", or "Try to beat up some nice young girls and end up a cripple eh, oh dear oh dear oh dear". Nothing would stay a secret for very long amongst the locals. Jim had to just walk by and take it on the chin, what choice did he have?

Walking towards him Jim saw someone who appeared to be in as bad a state as he was, it was Andrew and he was also out in an attempt to walk off the morning stiffness. "Andrew, I see that you are feeling it this morning as well."

"Hi Jim, what me, no I feel fine." Andrew tried to stride forward to hide the stiffness, "Oh bugger that bloody hurt," he cried as he came to a stop.

"I think that answers my question mate, don't worry I feel just as bad. Darcy certainly gave us a good workout didn't she?"

"You're not wrong, I'm in bloody agony to be honest." The locals could not help noticing the two of them together. "I've only got one wheelchair, you will have to take it in turns to push each other", or "You will never be a match for those girls, why don't you give it up?" Andrew and Jim turned to each other, give it up, this was not going to be an option. They did not need to say anything to each other, that comment made them even more determined to carry on. They would be there on Friday for more pain, the hard work had only just started.

Jim continued on the way to Sharon's as was the routine, it just took a little more time than usual. During the walk he couldn't help thinking that he wanted to get back in the pool and practise some of the things Darcy had shown them. Friday seemed to be a long way off. When Jim arrived at the house Sharon seemed to be in quite a good mood.

"Oh 'ere he is, the other beautiful man in my life, well apart from my Barry of course, come in there's a cup of tea waiting for you. Are you alright? You're walking all funny, never mind sit down in the kitchen." Jim didn't bother explaining why he was feeling a bit stiff, he just did what he was told and sat by the tea that was there waiting for him.

"You will not believe this Jim, John was up early this morning, went straight to college and he was singing 'Isn't She Lovely' all morning and all the way up the road, singing out loud I tell you. I didn't know what had come over him at first but then I realised, it's love Jim." Sharon then attempted a joke, "It's love Jim but not as we know it," if you have watched *Star Trek* you should recognise the reference. Sharon thought she was being very witty and had a good laugh at her own joke.

"What do you mean Sharon?" Jim pretended to have no knowledge of John's crush on Darcey. Sharon paused and then looked at Jim with a face full of pride. "I thought it must be that girl at your swimming at first, OK he might fancy her a bit, but I think it has brought out his love for his old mum, he is being really good to me, he loves his mum bless his heart." Jim smiled with a sense of relief, "Of course he does." It was for the best Sharon thought that.

Before Jim had a chance to finish his cup of tea he was given the list of jobs for the morning. It was typical that they would involve either bending down or trying to get into a small gap somewhere, just when Jim was not feeling at his most flexible. The first job was to look at a blockage that had led to the kitchen sink draining very slowly, a simple enough job but it was going to hurt Jim's aching body for sure. He wasn't going to tell Sharon that the job might be too much for him, there was no point in inviting the mockery that would follow, he just slowly got down to the kitchen floor so he could open the cupboard underneath the sink and see what the cause of the blockage was. There were more than a few groans as Jim got down on all fours.

"What's the matter with you, Jim, you sound knackered and you have hardly started!"

"I'm OK, how long has it been blocked for then?"

"Well ever since I washed what was left of John's chilli and rice down the sink, bless him it's one of his favourites, he loves his old mum, strange though he didn't finish it, it was like his mind was on something." Jim was still not telling Sharon fully about what was going on with John, he was just amazed that Sharon would be so careless, no surprise that the sink was blocked!

"The bloody u-bend will be blocked then won't it, blocked with chilli, you stupid woman... aarrr my bloody back."

"Well get on and fix it then instead of giving me this abuse, it's like you think it was my fault or something, what's a bloody u-bend anyway?" Jim cleared the cupboard and got the u-bend off quite quickly despite the agony he was feeling, he had made sure he could catch any water in a washing up bowl. Once it was off Jim showed Sharon how it was full of the remains of John's tea. "That's a bloody u-bend and it's bloody blocked."

"OK don't get excited, it is a good job you are here to fix it then Jim. I'll leave you to it if you can manage." Sharon left to watch TV in the lounge. It was better that Jim was left alone to struggle to his feet without Sharon looking over him.

Jim was careful to clear the blockage catching any water from the tap in the bowl he was using. It was when he was back under the sink about to put the u-bend back on when Dot came into the kitchen. She saw Jim on the floor. "Morning Jim I see Sharon has got you working again." Dot saw the bowl full of dirty water in the sink and poured it down the plughole. "Who left that there then? What the sodding hell are you doing?" Jim rose quickly from beneath the sink his head covered in dirty water.

"My bloody back," he got up too quickly. "I'm all wet and my bloody back hurts."

"Jim, mind your language, don't you speak to me like that."

"Sorry, Mum, but look at me."

"Yes you're all wet and look at the mess you have made over my nice clean kitchen." Dot left and joined Sharon in the lounge. "He is in a right mood today, moaning and groaning like an old man. Come and see this bloke on TV, he has just found out his girlfriend is a man!" Jim was left to finish the job and clear up the mess, there was little point in arguing about it.

After Jim had completed the few jobs he had been given that morning there was still no concern shown from Sharon or Dot for the pain he was in, although he was feeling better and putting it on a bit at the end just to try and get some sympathy.

"Thanks Jim, see you tomorrow then, you better be in a better mood, all that moaning and groaning, you're not fit, you need to take more exercise!" Jim controlled the urge to react and just waved as he left the house. 'More bloody exercise,' he thought to himself, what he had just done had nearly crippled him. However he was walking more easily on his way home, maybe more exercise and practice could be the answer. It might be a nice surprise for Darcy if she could see that they were having a crack at this synchronised swimming lark. Jim decided that he would get back in the pool today for some extra training. It was home to get his swimming gear and then straight to the pool then.

Jim was surprised when he got to the pool that it was actually quite busy, the local school had just turned up for a session and were just going in to get changed as Jim approached the ticket office. “One adult swim please.” There was a pause and a look of disgust from the girl behind the counter.

“You what?”

“I said one adult swim please.”

“Are you some sort of perv or something, this is a school’s session, you want to get in with the schoolkids do you?” It was quite understandable that Jim took exception to this.

“No, I just want a bloody swim, that’s all, just a bloody swim.”

“Well you can’t, the school is in for the next hour and a half.”

“Can I go up to the balcony and wait for them to finish?” The look from the girl pretty much gave the answer. “You want to watch the schoolkids do you?”

Jim got the message, “No I bloody don’t, I will come back this afternoon if there is no risk of being arrested!”

“Oh, OK, the water should be alright by about two o’clock, the kids tend to piss in the pool, I wouldn’t go in the pool just after that lot.” Jim left with the question in his head, were the kids weeing whilst in the pool or weeing in the pool from the side; he did not want to dwell on that so he left but determined to come back in the afternoon.

After quite a light lunch Jim was back at the pool, the same girl was behind the ticket counter. “One adult swim please, if that’s OK, I don’t want you to call the police or anything.” The girl looked very unimpressed and just took Jim’s money; without saying a word she shoved a ticket back in Jim's direction. Once changed Jim entered the pool area to find it virtually empty, just three others in there. He took a look at the water following his visions of what the kids might have done earlier that morning but it looked OK. It was safe to go ahead so Jim got himself into the water. At first it was just a couple of lengths to warm up, then it was time to remember what Darcy had taught them and to put in some practice.

The various moves that Jim was making didn't go unnoticed by the others in the pool. There were a few curious glances turning into long stares of disbelief. What was a grown man doing that for, is he right in the head? Yes he was right in the head, he was training and considering what he looked like didn't feel like a fool at all. It was going well, he remembered more than he thought he would, twirling and splashing about with about as much grace as you would reasonably expect. Of course it would occasionally go wrong, the others in the pool either laughed or called him a stupid git under their breath.

Jim was so carried away with his routines that he did not notice the bright orange swimsuit entering the pool, not to mention who was wearing it. "Hello Jim, like the moves." It was Tilly. Jim looked up, surprised to see Tilly there.

"Oh, hi, what are you doing here?"

"Well that's a welcome. I suppose I am here for the same reason as you."

"What do you mean?"

"I thought I should get in a sneaky practice, great minds think alike it seems."

They both had plans for a quiet practice without anyone knowing, no chance of that it would appear. Well the only sensible thing to do was to practise the routines together, so

Tilly got in the water and they worked out what they were going to do. There were even more disapproving glances from the others in the pool and the occasional comment as Jim and Tilly twirled, splashed, dived and glided across one end of the pool. "They must be bonkers" or "They're taking over the bloody pool now!" Jim was not happy with that last comment considering what he was fighting against, with Julie trying to do just that, take over the pool.

"We are not taking over the pool, there is room for all of us." Well looking around the pool, it wasn't very busy. Tilly was not about to let this situation develop and just grabbed Jim, "Never mind them we've got work to do!" So the workout continued despite the protests.

The routine came to a point where Jim held Tilly and instead of breaking for a twirl or a dive their eyes met. At this point you may want to again imagine some romantic music because they kissed, and I mean a proper kiss. The feelings they obviously had for each other were hard to control. By this time the pool attendant was taking an interest. "You over there, no petting, no petting in the pool." Another man who was having a swim had other ideas as he closed in on his wife.

"Get off me Gerald, that means you too!"

Jim and Tilly had not broken their clinch and the attendant was about to try to separate them with one of those long poles you find at the pool when there was another familiar voice.

"Hit them with that and I will shove it right up your arse mate!" It was Cath, and yes she meant what she said. That was more than enough for the attendant to back off. Jim and Tilly broke their clinch to see her looking smugly in their direction.

"Caught you at it then."

"Err, we were just practising."

"Yes it looks like it."

Tilly looked at Cath with a sheepish grin, "Yes Cath, just practising our routines. Anyway why are you here?"

"A quiet practice without you lot knowing, chance would be a fine thing; good job I turned up when I did, you were about to rip each other's costumes off you naughty buggers." Jim felt a little embarrassed, as did Tilly but she did not show it.

"Shut up and get in the pool Cath, we have work to do." Cath joined them in the pool giving Tilly a knowing smile, she did not need to say anything, she was happy that a good friend had found happiness. Cath hadn't known Jim for long but she saw him as a good sort so they could rip each other's costumes off in the pool with her blessing as far as she was concerned.

So there were now three of them practising the routines Darcy had shown them, the others in the pool were growing tired of making fun or directing comments at them and just got on with their swim (if you could call it that). It was not long, before as if in perfect synchronisation, Derek and Doris entered the pool from their respective changing rooms. "So much for our secret training Derek." There was nothing else but to join the rest and work on the same stuff. "Nice to see you all. I don't think you will see Steve or Andrew though, they wouldn't do this extra practice thing, never in a million years, they wouldn't would they Derek?"

"Well my love, don't be so sure."

"Shut up, Derek you know I'm right."

"I think you may be mistaken my sweet."

"Don't be silly, I keep telling you—"

"Have a bloody look woman!"

Doris looked up to see both Steve and Andrew standing by the poolside. "What in the name of arse is going on here?"

"Came in for a sneaky practice did you, Andrew?" asked Jim.

"Did I fuck, I just wanted a swim; pardon my language girls."

"That's not quite true is it Andrew, what was it you said as we arrived? 'Let's get a head start on the others and run through the routine, we will surprise them next session'; that's what you said isn't it?"

Steve had no hesitation in dropping Andrew in it. "Cheers mate, you could have kept your mouth shut."

So the whole group was there going through the routines, making plenty of mistakes but slowly getting the hang of it, it was hard work though with the odd grumble or argument. It was clear however that what they all wanted was to surprise Darcy and show her that they could actually do this and could give this competition a good go. Not just for themselves, but for Darcy, they all would like to wipe the sarcastic smiles off the faces of Julie and her group.

12

It's starting to come together

It was time for the next of the 'scheduled' practice sessions and Jim was looking forward to giving Darcy a surprise at what they could now do, no doubt the rest of the group were feeling the same way. On the way to the pool the various members of the group could be seen going through their moves not caring how ridiculous they looked, dancing and spinning down the road. Well Cath still managed to flip the back of a couple of kid's heads who were giving her a few cheeky comments, but still with a flowing grace, as if it was part of the routine.

Jim arrived outside the pool just as Stan was dropping Julie off. As soon as Julie saw Jim it was clear that she was giving Stan the full force of her frustration that the pool was not all hers. You could almost see the car rocking about with the fluffy dice swaying from side to side as Julie flung her arms about. From the body language, it was obvious that Stan was trying to say there was nothing more he could do without risking a police enquiry, which didn't seem to help much – couldn't Stan fix the police as well? After all this was for Julie! When Julie saw that Jim was watching the whole thing she stopped in her tracks, put on a forced smile, gave Stan a kiss and got out of the car.

"Hello Jim, nice to see you again. Going in with your friends again, well that's nice, see you in there, bye." Julie was never good at hiding the fact she was spoilt and two-faced. Jim turned to Stan as he drove off, there was a sort of resigned look of 'why me?' on Stan's face.

On approaching the ticket window two of Julie's girls pushed past Jim giggling; it was clear that sporting respect was not high on their priority list.

"Don't worry about them Jim, they're both useless and stupid!"

It was Darcy who had just arrived. The two girls just huffed and giggled a little bit more before going through to the changing rooms.

"Hi Jim, are you ready for our session? Let's see how much we can remember from last time." Jim was bursting to tell Darcy about all the extra practice they had been putting in but no, they should surprise her.

"I hope we don't let you down, Darcy."

"Let me down; don't be daft, just do your best that's all I ask." She meant that but she did want to have at least a chance to take Julie down a peg or two. "Come on, Jim, let's show 'em what we can do, eh?" Darcy gave Jim a motivating nudge on his shoulder.

Just as Darcy made her way to the female changing room to get changed and wait for the girls John walked in. He seemed embarrassed to see Jim there. "Err… hello fancy seeing you here."

"What do you mean fancy seeing me here, what are you doing here? Come to give us some support have you?"

"Err, yes, I suppose."

"Well that's nice, nice to see you." By this time Tilly, Andrew and Cath had also arrived. "That's nice isn't it? John has come to give us some support."

"Come because of Darcy more like, he is not here for us

Jim." Tilly appeared to be right as John's face was looking a little red. Jim was actually quite pleased: "John you little rascal."

"I bet he is a little rascal as well."

"Behave yourself, Cath," Tilly told her off; poor John's face was now even redder. John could not wait to get away and hurried up the stairs to the viewing gallery. It would appear that John and Darcy had seen each other a few times now, away from the attentions of Sharon. The rest approached the ticket office window to buy their tickets. The girl behind the counter was now resigned to the fact they were allowed in but still didn't like it.

"Oh God it's the bloody old fogies again."

One stern look from Cath and the girl hurried into a bit more action and issued the tickets, handing out more change than they were due! It was definitely better to have Cath with you on your team than against you.

They left the changing rooms for the pool, only to be met by a reception of focused glares from Julie and her girls; a couple of them forgot the brief and started to giggle before they were brought back into line. This was really quite pathetic as you would imagine and certainly did not have the desired effect. Tilly could not resist.

"Nice to see you again Julie, so nice we can all get along."

Andrew just enquired, "Haven't you seen a man in trunks before luv?"

If the tactic was to intimidate Jim and the group out of the pool this did not stand a chance. Just then there was a cry from the balcony, "Come on Darcy show 'em what you can do." To which Darcy smiled and waved back up to John. The group first looked at John and then at Darcy, as they both smiled at each other and gave a little loving wave.

So much for the group's surprise for Darcy, this was quite a surprise for them, especially Jim although he was quite pleased.

"Right, you heard him: let's show them what we can do."

Darcy broke her eye contact with John to take control of the session.

As they went through what they had practised Darcy could not believe what she was seeing, they actually showed signs of being able to do this. There was a grace and flow to the spins and dives making it look almost effortless – a bit like swans looking elegant on the surface with the legs going like bugger under the surface.

"This is brilliant, at this rate we will do well in the competition up at the Crystal Palace pool, this is really good."

Julie had also noticed that they were doing better than she would have liked and also that they would be competing against them in the competition. She looked a bit concerned and was not prepared for a fair fight. Julie left the pool area clutching her phone. Ten minutes later she returned with a sly smile on her face. "Come on girls we have a competition to train for."

It was about half an hour into the session when Stan and some bloke dressed as if he had just been taken off a golf course entered the poolside. Julie stopped the session, gaining the attention of everybody, "Right Stan, let Mr Sims tell this lot the rules of entry for this competition and see how they like it!"

All eyes were on this Mr Sims who appeared to be one of the competition officials. "Well you will be aware that for most synchronised swimming contests all the competitors need to be, how can I say, female." Jim and the group looked deflated whereas Julie was looking very smug. But

Mr Sims had not finished. "'I have checked the rules for this particular contest and have to say that I can see no such rule, so both these teams can enter. Can we get back to our game of golf now, I was beating you wasn't I?" Julie's face dropped like a stone and started to fill with rage. Stan left in a hurry as if to make a run for it. Mr Sims turned to Darcy and mouthed 'good luck' and the group laughed in relief. So the competition was on and there was nothing Julie could do about it. Stan might be in for a hard time if he dared to go home!

The session went well; things were coming together and even though it was hard work the group had smiles on their faces (this is as important as the make-up for the presentation of the performance I believe). Even though Darcy began to have hope that they may be competitive she was not going to show it and asked for more work from the group. Julie took this a sign that they were not doing that well and kept telling her girls how much better they were. Sure Julie was worried, she wasn't used to having to work or fight for what she wanted, but she was still confident that 'her girls' were a class above and with a bit more work they would make sure that Jim and the rest wouldn't be a threat. Julie would add the occasional comment across the pool, intended to wind up Jim and the others, but this had little effect, apart from keeping their smiles up. It was great to be getting under Julie's skin to be honest.

After the session the group were very tired but their spirits were high. Andrew was straight off to the pub and it did not take much to persuade Steve and Cath to join him. Tilly was in discussion with Derek and Doris, they knew about Sharon's obsession with Barry Manilow and with their connections Tilly's son was working on a bit of a surprise for the competition. They offered their excuses about going for a drink; they were tempted but were almost dead on their feet. After all, they were in training – there would be plenty of time for drinking after the competition. On his way home Jim felt he could not resist calling in on Sharon to tell her about John's new girlfriend. It was a bit of a surprise but Jim was happy for his nephew.

When he got there the front door opened before he had a chance to knock the knocker.

"Look who it is, the highly tuned sportsman, looking so pleased with yourself. I want to have word with you, get in and sit under my Barry!"

"Evening Sharon and how are you?" Jim knew he would not have a chance to tell his news, he was going to be under interrogation first for something or other. He was ushered to the place he least liked to sit, under the picture of Barry Manilow: you could not look up to avoid the attentions of Sharon as the view up Barry's nose was worse.

"What have you got to say for yourself then?" Jim was unsure how to respond, what did he have to answer to this time? "My John has suddenly taken up a strong interest in swimming but never takes a swimming costume with him, what is going on?"

"He's turned that pool into a knocking shop with nude swimming that's what it is."

"Quiet, Mum."

Dot was already sitting in the lounge and was not afraid of getting straight to the point. "Well is it true, is it naked frolics in the pool? No wonder you have always got a smile on your face these days. He calls it a community swimming club, community sex club more like."

"Mum stop, this is my little boy you're talking about."

"Not so little by all accounts, reminds me of your father!"

"I don't believe this, we are synchronised swimmers and proud of it," protested Jim. It was still not the sort of thing you would expect him to say.

"We train hard, with our costumes on Mum, we have our contest to work for."

"As for John I think he has taken a bit of a shine to Darcy but there are no naked frolics in the pool, to be honest I am pleased for him."

"In that case you will be pleased to know he has her up in his room now."

Jim was quite surprised at what Sharon had to say.

"Soon we will start hearing the bed springs, reminds me of your father."

"Oh please, Mum, we don't want to know about that."

At that moment John and Darcy came down the stairs and entered the lounge.

"You got dressed quick!"

"Stop Mum! Hello Darcy, everything OK?" Sharon was trying to show her polite side. Jim was still surprised to see Darcy there. "Hello Darcy, nice to see you and John getting on." He then looked at John who had a smug but slightly embarrassed look on his face. "You're a dark horse, good for you," giving him a playful nudge on the shoulder with a bit of a chuckle. Darcy, also looking a little bit embarrassed, announced that she had to go and that it was nice to see everyone. Dot mumbled that she had seen quite a lot of one person in particular but no notice was taken of her. Darcy gave John a kiss at the door and started to leave. John saw the three of them ready to question him and decided, quite rightly, to leave with Darcy and walk her home.

"John, where are you going? Come back I have something

to ask you." That was what he was afraid of, he would sneak in later to try and avoid being caught by the interrogation Sharon had planned for him. Jim knew what would come next and left before Sharon started on him. "See you soon, must go now."

"Jim come back I've not finished with you." Too late. Jim had escaped and was walking down the street.

Not for the first time recently Jim had a spring in his step, things were turning out OK. There was the swimming which had brought some focus to his life, Tilly who had brought some romance to his life and seeing John finding what could be love brought joy to his life. Yes, he knew there was plenty of hard work ahead for the competition but things were turning out OK.

The next swimming sessions were hard work and at times the group had moments of doubt that they could do it. All it took was a word from someone, usually Cath, to bring the group back in line. "Shut up and do that fucking spin before I punch you in the face!" Even some girls in Julie's group would start spinning at random times in fear of Cath much to Julie's annoyance. John would be there in the gallery, sometimes joined by Sharon so she could see what was going on. What Sharon saw was a good deal of hard work and both her brother and son finding a bit of romance, dare I say it, love. They were however getting better each time, they were beginning to look forward to the competition with some confidence.

13

This is what we have been working for!

It was the morning of the competition and Jim was full of nervous excitement; after the hard work they had all put in this meant a lot to the group. They did not want to let themselves, or more to the point, each other down. As Jim walked down Maple Road there was a definite buzz in the air. It would be nice to think that this was in anticipation of the grand synchronised swimming contest, but no chance, people didn't seem at all interested in that. It happened to also be FA Cup Final day and by some miracle Crystal Palace were playing Chelsea for the cup (I did say this was a work of fiction). There were red and blue banners and balloons dressed in most of the windows and a great feeling of optimism.

"Come on you Eagles, eh, Jim, the boys are going to do it I know they are!" Jim sort of knew the person who now had his arm round him waiting for a response. "Well Jim, are you going to the pub to watch it? We are going to thrash Chelsea, who do they bloody think they are, eh?" Jim was unsure how to respond.

"Bloody Chelsea, need to be taken down a peg or two that lot." That seemed to be the right answer.

"Too right Jim, too bloody right." The man left satisfied with the answer giving Jim a pat on the shoulder. That did however remind Jim of another team who needed to be taken down a peg or two.

Jim arrived at Sharon's to find a full house. Along with Sharon, Dot and John there was Darcy and even Tilly was there.

"We have been waiting for you." Tilly welcomed Jim with the usual smile and bright coloured top. "Sharon has a proper breakfast for us, give us the strength for this afternoon, come and sit down." True enough there was porridge followed by bacon and eggs.

"Good for your energy, get it down you."

"Thanks Sharon, I may get used to this."

"Don't push your luck."

Darcy leant over the table. "So are we ready for this then?"

Jim was first to respond, "You bet we are Darcy. Can't wait."

"That's good Jim because we have something to arrange for you."

"What's that then Tilly?"

"Your make-up!"

After he had stopped choking on his bacon Jim protested, "What sodding make–up?"

"We all have to wear make–up it's part of the presentation, maybe some sequins as well."

"You must be kidding."

"No, we are doing it after breakfast."

There was no escape. John was lapping it up, "They will make you nice and pretty don't you worry."

Dot was more direct, "You're going to look like a right poof."

Jim was captive in the chair whilst Darcy and Tilly went to work on him. He was trying desperately not to show that he was quite enjoying the experience whilst the rest made it far too obvious that they found this highly amusing.

"You will never get the others here for this you know, not a chance. Oh you've missed a bit."

Tilly smiled at Darcy and then turned to Jim. "No need to, Doris is doing Derek and Cath has tricked Steve and Andrew to hers for, what was it, surplus home-made wine that needs a home. When they get there they might need some because Cath will not let them go until they're both done!"

"Poor buggers," Jim chuckled at their fate.

"What about you, you've got to walk home like that to get your gear."

Sharon was right, the walk up a busy Maple Road in full make-up may be a problem for the attention he would get.

When Jim was done, Tilly had agreed to walk with him as he went home, she was going that way anyway as the girls were all meeting Doris at her house so they could sort themselves out. This was clearly a well-executed plan to get the group ready, leaving no room for any makeover avoidance from anyone who may put up resistance (most likely the men). The walk back to Jim's flat was quite a short one but they did not go unnoticed, there was plenty of finger pointing and laughter. "Have a look at that!" or perhaps "I don't fancy yours much!"

Jim wasn't embarrassed; he walked Tilly hand in hand up the road, proud to be clad in more make-up than the woman that he loved. There was a brief look into each other's eyes, a little smile and they knew it didn't matter what people were saying. When they reached the flat, Tilly left Jim to sort out his kit for the competition and carried on to Doris's house to get ready.

"See you later. I won't kiss you right now, it will disturb

your sequins. Make sure you are there nice and early. Love you Jim." As Tilly left, Jim was close to being an emotional wreck, happy that Tilly loved him, nervous at the thought of the competition, how can a man find his trunks in these circumstances?

Jim was at the Crystal Palace National Sports Centre nice and early. They had agreed to all meet outside and go in together. Cath was already there.

"Hi Cath, you ready for this then?"

"Jim you look wonderful. You two, you can stop hiding now, Jim is here." Steve and Andrew emerged from behind a tree, made up almost like the ugly sisters. "You look lovely, all of you." It was not long before they had all arrived. All had their full make-up; it certainly was a sight and they all took comfort in thinking the others looked more ridiculous than themselves, having a friendly laugh at each other in the process. Darcy had also arrived and Sharon, Dot and John had come with her. Sharon insisted that John took a photo of the group; this was an image worth keeping. Dot for once just smiled – even though she had plenty of ammunition for a comment, there was a feeling of pride.

It was Darcy's job to go and pick the draw so they would know the order the teams would perform in.

"Oh for God's sake, let us go on first so we can get it over with."

"It will be OK Cath, just enjoy it."

Tilly was just as nervous but did not want to show it.

"Let's go first so I can go and watch Palace in the final."

"If you mention that again I am going to rip your balls off!" Steve had found a way to calm Cath's nerves. Darcy was soon back with the draw.

"Well there are eight teams and we are on fifth; that's

alright, no that's good, the best place to be, trust me." Darcy then mentioned that Julie's team were on straight after them.

"Don't worry about them." The group were a bit taken aback but focused; they thought they had something that would be difficult for Julie and her girls to follow.

The competition had started and there was quite a good number of spectators in, more than expected and there was a buzz in the air. There were quite a few locals there, even David Bowie was spotted, supporting someone he knew. The audience seemed to be expecting something other than the synchronised swimming, well there were a few rumours going around. The group were all changed and ready, their costumes as bright as their make-up, only Tilly who normally wore a brighter costume commented that it lacked sparkle. Tilly turned to Derek and Doris: "Is he here then?" There was a nod and a wink in return. The connections in the show business world had somehow arranged for the song they were using for their routine to be sung live by the person who had made it famous. This was going to be quite something.

The first few performances went on and the standard was quite high. Each team gave Jim and the group a few curious glances as they passed in the waiting area, for some reason they did not expect to be competing against people like that! It was now their turn and they made their way to the poolside as the announcement was made.

"And now a group from Penge appearing for their first competition … oh and to sing the song live, we have Barry Manilow!"

It was true, he was there, white suit and big nose, there to sing their song. There were cheers from the expectant crowd. Sharon was in a state of shock. "It's my Barry, John it's MY BARRY!"

The performance started and Barry sang 'I write the songs that make the whole world sing'. It was a beautiful moment and the performance was as good as they could have hoped. The moves worked, they had wonderful flow and dare I say it, they were even synchronised. The faces of the judges had turned from the initial shock to almost reaching for the tissues. At the key change, two of the judges could not help standing up along with Barry and half the spectators. When they finished they were all relieved that it was now done. Darcy was so proud of what they had achieved. The crowd cheered, it was like something they had never seen before and in a weird sort of way they loved it. It was a unique performance, they played it to their strengths and didn't attempt what they clearly shouldn't attempt – it could not have gone better. The judges were left a little confused on how to mark it, however. They passed Julie and her girls as they left the pool, who looked like they were already beaten, how were they to follow that? The scores, however, were only to be announced after every group had performed.

Jim and the team did not return to the pool to watch the remaining performances but heard a loud cheer as Julie's group finished. Moments later they saw them return to the changing area with smug faces. Julie looked over, "Better luck next time, if they let you try again, they loved our routine." Even Cath felt it was best just to ignore her. It was soon time for all the groups to return to the poolside to hear the results; there was tense anticipation in the air. After what seemed to be a lot of unnecessary delay they were ready to read the results. Nobody spoke, there was too much tension.

"We will name the top three in reverse order."

There was a pause.

"In third place we have the Bathing Beauties from Penge."

Darcy screamed with delight. "What's that luv do you know them?"

"It's us Jim, we have got third place, we have only gone and got third place, go and get your cup!" The group were stunned, how could this be, they did not expect this. After the shock it was all hugs and kisses, how could this be true? Jim took Tilly with him to accept the cup; the crowd showed that they had enjoyed their performance. On their way back to the group they showed the cup to Julie, she did not appear to be that impressed and certainly not that pleased. Sharon, Dot and John screamed and cheered. When the group calmed down a bit Steve asked, "What's all this Bathing Beauties stuff about then?" Darcy replied that she had to give a name with the entry, and that was it. The announcer was ready to complete the results. Julie was looking confident that she must be first or at least second.

"In second place, the Catford Cats." Julie thought she must be first. "In first place," there was a pause, "the Beckenham Belles."

Julie's face dropped like a stone, she would later find out that they came fifth. Stan was seen making a quick exit as he would not want Julie to find him at this particular moment. You could see that Julie and her girls were gutted as they started arguing amongst themselves, their tears making streaks in their make-up and putting their sequins firmly out of place.

Jim was confused as to why there was a cheer after Julie's group had performed and yet they hadn't done as well as they thought. It turned out that Crystal Palace had scored at that precise moment (some of the crowd had radios). Julie's group had actually had a pretty poor performance – no amount of make-up could cover up that. Crystal Palace went on to win the FA Cup Final that day, what a day for Penge (like I said this is a work of fiction). The group changed, feeling on top of the world, and agreed to meet up later for a celebration drink and how they deserved it, they had done it alright. It was quite beyond what any of them thought possible at the start.

They all left to go home and ready themselves for the drink-up later that evening. Jim and Tilly walked back through Crystal Palace Park. There were kids playing football in Palace colours pretending they had also won the cup and various happy but drunk locals singing with their hands in the air. Jim and Tilly just held hands, feeling very contented and walked on through. When they reached Maple Road the market traders all noticed; news had reached them of their result in the pool. They all, in turn, stopped what they were doing, turned towards the happy couple and clapped, even Willy Plonker stopped shouting at some kid who had upset him in some way and joined with the applause. They all seemed to appreciate what they had achieved, sticking up for themselves and putting Julie in her place.

It was true, they had made their voice heard and would not stand for an absurd misuse of power; they would not see Julie and her girls back in their pool that's for sure. Come on you Bathing Beauties.

14

Back to the old routine then!

Later that evening they were all in the pub as they had arranged. It was still sinking in just what they had achieved.

"Bloody brilliant, just bloody brilliant, did you see the look on her face?"

They all agreed with Steve and there was a satisfying nod around the group. Jim turned to Darcy and raised his glass, "To the best coach we could have ever hoped for, thank you so much for making this happen."

"It was you, you did it. I just gave you the push you needed; they said that's how I should do it on my motivation course!" Whether you believe in these courses or not they certainly had a shared common purpose and it seemed to have worked.

Suddenly the pub door crashed open, it was Sharon along with John and Dot.

"It was my Barry! I don't believe it, he was here, in Penge!" As she approached the group Sharon did not notice who else was sitting at the table.

The guest stood up and with open arms said, "Hi Sharon. I have been told all about you, is there a song you would like me to sing to you?"

It takes a lot to silence Sharon but the one and only Barry Manilow asking her for a personal request in the local pub did the trick. Once she caught her breath she sat down next to her idol, still in a state of shock, who would have thought it?

John sat down next to Darcy, giving her a big hug. "That was fantastic." This was a good time, quite right to celebrate and enjoy the moment. Some bright spark put a Manilow song on the jukebox and even Jim started to sing along. This was a special evening and they were going to make sure they enjoyed themselves.

So what happened next you may ask?

Well the group still meet for their regular sessions without any problems from Julie, she is keeping a lower profile now. They still practice a few moves now and then, just for a bit of fun more than anything else. They do not intend to enter any more competitions. They had their pool back and that meant a great deal.

John and Darcy are still together, a case of young love, events that have changed John for the better. He has turned from teenager to young man.

Sharon is now emailing her idol Barry and receives regular replies; there is talk of going out to Las Vegas to meet up with him again. Sharon is hoping that they will be going to the chapel so Elvis can marry them, but this is not likely.

And what of Jim and Tilly? Well, they are very much a couple and living a happy life together. Sharon does not feel the need to arrange any further blind dates.

All of the group are now respected a little bit more in the community for what they have done, not that this is shown much. There is still a fair bit of banter.

It is back to the same routine of daily walks and the DIY for Jim but now with Tilly in his life, it could not ever quite be the same again, but in a good way. I don't think Penge will ever be the same again.

About the Author

I was born in 1966 in Beckenham, a leafy suburb of South East London, just in time to wave a rattle when England won the World Cup. Being my parents' fourth child I was born at home, a place I lived in for the next twenty-two years. Beckenham still holds fond memories from childhood. The wonderful playground that was our large and wild back garden and childhood friends with whom I still keep in touch.

As with most of my family the call of the West Country was hard to resist and I moved to near Bristol in 1999. Bristol and the surrounding area I have known well from frequent visits to my grandparents. It is now like living somewhere you associate with being on holiday, yet you are still in touch with London when you want to be. I live just outside Bristol with my wife Sarah.

I thank you for reading my story and hope that you enjoy it.